# Pangyrus

ISBN: 978-0-9979164-2-3


Printed in the United States of America
First published in 2018



The text of this book is set in Palatino
with display text set in Crimson and Baskerville
Composition by Yahya Chaudhry and Abraar Chaudhry
Cover design by Douglas Woodhouse



Pangyrus
79 JFK Street, L103
Cambridge, MA 02138
pangyrus.com

# *Contents*

# Pangyrus

# *Note from the Editor*

I was talking recently with Deb Norkin, editor of *Zest!*, our new food section. Both of us felt *Pangyrus* was overdue for a writing contest.

"Why not food and resistance?" I asked--thinking we'd combine the contest with Resistance Mic!, our collaboration with the Carr Center for Human Rights Policy at Harvard and the American Repertory Theater. "The contest winners could get on stage at the Oberon and..."

She reacted as if I'd suggested something like sharpened tostadas whipped, Oddjob style, at dictators. "Not everyone will have a story of that."

It wasn't long, though, before everyday examples came to mind. Just in my own family, the cycle of Jewish holidays put before us every year matzoh, recalling the struggle of slavery; hamentaschen, three-cornered cookies that warn of ethnic cleansing; and latkes, potato pancakes whose oil commemorates guerilla warfare against foreign occupiers. Claudia Rodin, in *The Book of Jewish Food,* presents "Almodrote de Berengena," an eggplant flan so beloved among Sephardic Jews that they refused to give it up even though it gave them away. The Court of the Inquisition viewed its presence in a home as evidence the family was only pretending to be Christian.

The stories aren't all so historic. My brother and I grew up in a state of cereal warfare, using boxes of Life and Cheerios to build walls at breakfast. My father, facing the eternal parental challenge of getting his sons to eat Brussels sprouts, achieved a famous, but Pyrrhic, victory: the sprouts came back up along with the rest of dinner.

The more Deb and I thought about it, the more we saw everyone has foods of conflict, and foods of consensus. Foods that represent a boundary between 'us' and 'them'—and foods that transgress boundaries. To take in food is to take in stories. It's hard to say which nurtures us more, the calories or the culture. And as much as we take in, we never know it all, never see all the human effort and history that supplied the table, or brought us to sit at it.

This is what makes work at a journal like Pangyrus so exciting: that there is no end to stories, no end to surprising connections. This spring sees not only the launch of *Zest!* and our first contest, not only Resistance Mic!, but a new science section as well. And let's not forget "Ask Annie," fiction editor Anne Bernays's advice column on writing.

Three and a half years after *Pangyrus* debuted, in other words, we're innovating and growing. We owe a tremendous debt of gratitude for your support, and for the work of the editors and the authors who made this volume (and all our publications) possible. When we began I could not have imagined the conversations we'd start, or the community we'd gather. Now I don't have to imagine it: I encounter the evidence every day. And if you're reading us, you will, too. Turn the page, and enjoy!

—Greg Harris, Editor

# WHY WE BREAK OUR STUFF ACCIDENTALLY-ON-PURPOSE

aturing JENGA
d a COFFEE MUG
OSH'17
HUMAN BEINGS ARE STRANGE, AND WE FEEL THE NEED TO JUSTIFY OUR BEHAVIORS.
THOUGH WE THINK OF OURSELVES AS RATIONAL HUMAN BEINGS, WE ARE NOT.

HBS PROFESSOR FRANCESCA GINO WAS PART OF A RESEARCH TEAM THAT STUDIED WHY WE'RE SO CARELESS WITH OUR PRODUCTS.
SILVIA BELLEZZA
JOSH ACKERMAN
FRANCESCA GINO

THEY FOUND THAT WE TEND TO CONSUME PRODUCTS MORE **QUICKLY** AND USE THEM MORE **WASTEFULLY** WHEN AN **"UPGRADE"** IS AVAILABLE.
FOR EXAMPLE, WE'RE LESS LIKELY TO LOOK FOR A LOST CELLPHONE--OR FIX ONE THAT'S JUST SLIGHTLY DAMAGED--WHEN A NEW MODEL IS AVAILABLE.
OOPS! HOW **CLUMSY** OF ME. GUESS I GOTTA UPGRADE TO THAT NEW DEVICE NOW...
Perfectly good phone
THE TEAM USED DATASETS FROM A LOST-AND-STOLEN PHONE REGISTRY, AS WELL AS SELF-REPORTING, TO DRAW SOME CONCLUSIONS
IMEI DETECTIVE
Stolen, lost and found mobile phones and other devices
IMEI
Check if phone is stolen or lost
Search IMEI...
What is the IMEI number of ...?
Check how the system works
Anti theft phone applications
BUT THEY WANTED TO DOCUMENT THIS KIND OF CARELESSNESS IN A CONTROLLED SETTING.
I NEEDED TO CREATE AN ENVIRONMENT WHERE WE WERE ALLOWING PEOPLE TO TAKE **RISKS**.

THE BEGINNING OF THE STUDY,
THE RESPONDENTS WERE GIVEN
PLAIN **WHITE CERAMIC COFFEE**
G AND ASKED TO **EVALUATE** IT.

THIS IS A **GIFT** FOR YOU TO KEEP.

Rated 4.8 out of 10

BUT **HALF** THE SUBJECTS WERE TOLD...
YOU MAY HAVE THE OPPORTUNITY TO **PURCHASE** ONE OF THESE OTHER MUGS -- WHICHEVER IS YOUR **FAVORITE** -- AT A SPECIAL PRICE -- AT THE END OF THE STUDY.
Rated **6.0** out of 10

AND THEN THEY PLAYED **JENGA.**

IN THIS VERSION OF THE GAME THE GOAL WASN'T TO CONTINUE BUILDING THE TOWER--
The free mug

--BUT JUST TO REMOVE AS MANY BLOCKS AS POSSIBLE--WITH THE INCENTIVE OF BEING **PAID*** FOR EACH BLOCK REMOVED.
*Five cents per block!

BUT...
YOU ARE NOT ALLOWED
CATCH THE MUG IF IT FAL
AND YOU WON'T RECEIV
A NEW MUG IF YOURS **BREAKS.**

JENGA IS ALREADY A GAME ABOUT RISK. THE RESEARCHERS WANTED THE EXPERIMENT TO FEEL "**ESPECIALLY RISKY.**"

THE RESULTS? WHILE BOTH GROUPS REMOVED ABOUT 13 BLOCKS IN THE PROCESS OF PLAYING THE GAME, THE GROUP THAT HAD BEEN **OFFERED** THE NICER MUGS TIPPED THE TOWER ALMOST **TWO-THIRDS** OF THE TIME.

TWICE AS OFTEN AS THE "NO-UPGRADE" GROUP.

APPARENTLY, THE **IDEA** OF THOSE BETTER MUGS MADE THEM MORE CARELESS WITH THE LESSER MUG THEY ALREADY OWNED.

IT IS EASIER TO MAKE THA
PURCHASE OR UPGRADE WH
THE PRODUC
WE HAVE IS
**DAMAGED.**

TEAM BELIEVES THAT MORE
RMATION MAKES THE WORLD
BETTER PLACE.
KE PEOPLE TO BE AWARE OF THE
ANGE WAYS THEIR MINDS WORK.
PERHAPS THEY WILL BE MORE THOUGHTFUL IN THE FUTURE.

AND HOPEFULLY THIS NEW "ALT-JENGA" WON'T CATCH ON...

# *For I Will Consider My Friend Susan*

## *by Jill McDonough*

For she is the servant of the Living God,
and worships in her way. For this is done
by wiping her Countertops seven times over
with evident Quickness. For she worries
and plans, asks me to cut Onions for supper
in a Quarter-Inch Dice. For her concerns
are so evident on her face I am even willing
to cut Onions in a Quarter-Inch Dice. For this
she loves me, for she knows it is not of my Nature
to be precise, to bring precision to any first
draft, which is living, which is cutting up foods
to be consumed for suppertime. For she is a mixture
of gravity and Waggery, and even in her precision
finds a way to treasure me, though my sloppy little
spirit is such a Challenge to love: I forget my
toothbrush, forget my Pants, drink all the gin,
leave coffee rings, make more reasons to wipe
more Counters more times. For there is nothing
sweeter than her Peace when at rest, after two
gin and tonics on the green velvet sofa with a stringle,
pretzels, in front of a Vintage Antiques Road Show.

# *Love in a Cup*

## *by Priya Gupta*

"I'll have a chai," I say.

"You mean a chai tea latte?" my barista asks.

There is a long, uncomfortable pause that she doesn't seem to notice. "Fine," I say.

Chai. Tea. Latte. Most of my friends, and not just the close ones, know how acutely this causes me cultural indigestion.

In India, chai is inherently both tea and a "latte." Calling chai a chai tea latte is like calling a bagel a "bread bagel," but is somehow even more annoying. Seemingly, the Western packaging of this foreign item makes both the drink and the name easier to consume.

Although the exact preparation of chai varies as much as the people who make it (ginger today? Cardamom? Cinnamon? One type of tea leaf or two? When *exactly* does the milk go in?), what remains consistent is that chai is a ritual. It has families sitting and sipping together. It punctuates the day. It's an activity, an invitation, a shared pleasure. You invite people over "for chai" as an easier-than-dinner way to see them. You politely ask for "half a cup" when really you want the full thing. Your family finds itself "hooked up" on one type of tea leaf (my father's way of describing our collective dependence on Green Label tea) and panicking when it stops being distributed in your country. My sister describes it as "love in a cup."

And then a sugary abomination gets packaged and marketed in the name of this thing you hold so dear. And a bindi-wearing, henna-donning, just-got back-from-hot-yogaing North American asks you incredulously, "You know how to make chai tea? Cool!" It gives me reflux.

The introduction of Eastern cultural phenomena in the Western world is a long-standing phenomenon. Chinese character tattoos, green tea flavoured everything, Bollyfit. Introduction to new practices, and perhaps even fusion, are not necessarily cultural crimes. Culture is not static; it evolves. I acknowledge that tea came to India from China (the Hindi word "chai" comes from the Chinese "cha") and drinking it was promoted by the British. Yet in America there is a tendency to market items and ideas in a manner that abrades context and history, Chinese and British and Indian alike. When everything non-native is branded as exotica, it starts to feel like exploitation.

Picture this: I walk into a spacious room with wooden floors and swirly mystical symbols on the walls. The room is teeming with impossibly fit women wearing see-through tights and crop tops that say "Be The Change" —and of course the token man in a tank top, can't forget him—chattering away to each other about which brand of coconut water is the closest to blood plasma and therefore can be injected directly into the bloodstream. These philosophers are all various avatars of a pretzel. The set of a new Lululemon short film, you ask? Nope, it's Jungle Yoga class. What is Jungle Yoga, you ask? I'm about to find out. The teacher walks in and puts on some Radiohead, which somehow inspires everyone to sit cross legged and look meditative. As we move through an awkward sequence of postures the teacher says profound things like, "Get yourself to the edge of your cliff without jumping off. How can you be at the edge without letting yourself pop?" Um, what? She also instructs, "Picture your right foot forming an ink blot, and your lungs as huge empty caverns. But meditate! Don't think. Think about your breath. But don't think. Meditate through your body." Again…what? My mind is spinning by this time, thinking about the fact that I'm thinking and wondering what time it is. We all join in an ill-pronounced "Namaste" at the end. Does everyone feel more spiritual now?

Growing up with a mother who practiced and taught yoga did not prepare me for experiences such as that one. With and through my mother I learned that yoga was a spiritual discipline, about fostering honesty and purity in our thoughts, intentions, actions and physical body. The physical practice was only one of many limbs of yoga, used fundamentally as a way of preparing the body for long stretches of meditation. She started her classes for other women who had just emigrated from India like she did; they were of all shapes and sizes and none of them had practiced yoga before. Over time her classes have evolved to include all genders and ethnicities. They started off as simple and inclusive; they remain that way 30 years later. She includes *pranayama* (breath work), meditation, yoga philosophy and physical postures. Students wear loose comfortable clothing, and few can put their legs behind their heads. My experiences of yoga in India thus far have been similar, with the cultural and spiritual origins of the practice being inseparable from the physical, and teachings extending far beyond a mat on the floor of a studio.

Every interpretation of a cultural practice is exactly that – an interpretation. My mother's practice started as an extension of her father's and evolved based on teachers she met and extensive readings on yoga history and philosophy. My family's version of the perfect cup of chai takes into account our individual tastes and experimenting with the ingredients at our disposal. What makes a difference is the level of commitment in understanding the essence of something – a prayer, a practice, a ritual, a drink – and executing it in a way that respects its origins. I am not averse to cultural evolution, nor do I believe in cultural monopoly; I have taken many an inspiring yoga class with a non-Indian teacher. But the plain truth is that when a cultural practice is being borrowed, the commitment to understanding it needs to be strong, even more intentional than if one had grown up in its midst. Because if culture evolves faster than a colony of fruit flies, inarguably something will be lost. When the word chai is merely "a drink with a spice" and yoga is "all the ways you can get closer to your crotch than you ever thought possible," all that is really left is a tag – a word that is being used to promise a sense of authenticity. Although one could argue that an introduction into mainstream Western culture is a way to put a country or practice on the map of the global village we now live in, it can feel mighty disrespectful.

So next time you decide to try chai flavoured ice cream, hot vinyasa laughter yoga, or a Spiritual Gangster® cutoff with the Hindu God Ganesh on it, take it as inspiration to learn a little bit about that ancient diverse hot populous country 7,615 miles away.

Namaste.

# *Lesson from a Last Day*

## *by Mimi Schwartz*

My husband's living will is in his backpack when he checks into the little New England hospital near the lake house where we stay every summer. Not that we are worried. Stu has had mild pneumonia twice as a side effect of a weakened heart. The slight fever of the night before didn't stop him from playing Mexican Train with our granddaughter, Sara, the white-tiled dominoes standing and falling with their double laughter, her delight being his.

It is only the threat of a hurricane, one day away, that keeps us from going back to the lake house with oral antibiotics, as before. "With your heart condition," the clinic doctor warned, "if you run into trouble and the trees are down, you might not get here in time. Besides," he added, "IV antibiotics work more quickly than pills." With a big family party coming up next weekend, "quickly" sounded good, so Stu agreed, and now, a few minutes later, in comes the wheelchair.

Stu backs away. "I'll walk, thanks. I'm fine!"

The nurse, a blond with a winning smile, says, "Oh, come on, handsome!" and he climbs on, happily chatting, as she rolls him down the hall that connects clinic to hospital.

I stay to fill out forms, and when I get to Stu's room, he's already in bed. A dark-haired young man is in the middle of the room, introducing himself.

"I'm the hospitalist," he says in a clipped East Asian accent.

"What's that?" I ask, and he turns towards me.

"The hospitalist handles in-patient care," says Dr. K. His name is written on his white jacket. "I am in charge of your husband's treatment."

I try to loosen him up with a smile; Stu tries joking about the Red Sox game. No luck. So Stu says, "Just give him the living will—and the health proxy." We had started keeping copies in the glove compartment, just in case, so that the list of end-of-life protocols we *don't* want—resuscitation, antibiotics, oxygen, forced feeding—would protect us, ensuring death with dignity. Not like my grandmother, who spent ten years in a nursing home, blind and senile, because paramedics jumpstarted her heart at eighty-nine. Or like Stu's aunt who, despite severe Alzheimer's, had both legs amputated at eighty-six, a week before she died.

The hospitalist glances at the documents and gives them back. "So do you want the IV for intravenous antibiotics, or not?" He sounds annoyed.

"Of course, that's why we're here!"

"And should we do everything we can?"

"Of course. This is mild pneumonia, right?"

"Mild pneumonia, absolutely. But still I must ask." He writes something on the chart. What, I find out only later.

Stu asks for his backpack and gives Dr. K. his traveling medical record—a four-inch-thick history of cardioversion, ablations, EKGs, and echocardiograms since his heart attack in 1988—all ordered and backed by data on an Excel sheet. That's what engineering professors do. I hand Dr. K. a slip with Dr. R.'s cell phone number. "He's the cardiologist my husband sees up here. I called him and he says you can call anytime and he'll fill you in."

Dr. R. is connected to the big hospital, thirty miles north, and we thought of driving there until the local clinic doctor said: "You'll wait in the ER forever. Here, you'll be hooked up to antibiotics within an hour."

Not quite. The hospitalist first wants an echocardiogram, an EKG, and the results from blood work, so when our son comes two hours later, after his daughters' swim lesson, the nurse is just starting antibiotics plus oxygen, because Stu is feeling worse. Alan immediately asks about transferring Stu to the big hospital, but the hospitalist keeps saying, "It's just mild pneumonia. The antibiotics will soon kick in."

"What did Dr. R. say when you called?" I ask.

"I haven't called yet. Too busy." *This place is almost empty, you jerk.*

"But he's expecting your call." *You have time to order extra tests,* I want to shout, *and not to call the doctor who knows Stu's heart?* I resist. This hospitalist has the power, and we have no advocate here. At home in New Jersey, our doctor came every day after Stu's emergency appendectomy in May. He read Stu's charts, adjusted his meds, and kibitzed, as the two men have been doing for twenty years. If there was a hospitalist on duty, we never noticed.

By evening, Stu is feeling more chipper—and eating a cranberry scone that Alan brought. We all like Stu's nurse, a lively brunette who seems charmed by this upbeat, silver-haired, seventy-two-year-old patient.

"Go home. Get some rest! I'm going to sleep," Stu tells me, and the nurse nods in agreement.

So I leave, but when I call in the middle of the night, she tells me, "He's uncomfortable." I hurry back, taking the curves of our moonless dirt road as in daylight.

"Hi!" I say ten minutes later, as if I always drop by at 3 a.m.

"Hi!" Stu says, with effort. "You're here." His breath is raspy and I begin rubbing his back in large circles of rhythm, as I did in 1988, when he was in intensive care for three days after his heart attack. For twenty-two years, we have believed the back rubs saved him. "Umm. That's good!" Stu's breathing steadies and my fingertips find his spine and climb to his shoulders. "Keep that up all night!" He smiles, and so do I—until he can't seem to get comfortable lying down.

Stu's nurse used to be a cardiac nurse at the big hospital. She props more pillows under him and whispers to both of us: "You could make a formal request to transfer."

Nurses, I've found, know everything and tell you the truth, so I leave to look for the hospitalist. He's chatting at the nurses' station and I say, trying to be calmly authoritative: "I'm requesting that my husband be transferred to the big hospital. It is better equipped and his cardiologist is there."

The hospitalist scowls. He doubts that the hospital will admit anyone who is not an emergency, not with the hurricane coming. "Your husband is fine." And no, he hasn't contacted Dr. R. yet.

The sun is up when Alan arrives. His family is going back to Boston—school starts this week—but Alan says he'll stay awhile. I don't remember when the questions start. A small catheter would improve the delivery of antibiotics. Do we agree? Of course, if it will help. An intubation would help the breathing. Do we agree? I'm not sure what intubation involves, but yes, of course, if it will help. Stu is having more trouble breathing, and dozes more, but we still believe in mild pneumonia. No one says not to.

In fact, I don't really worry until—*Is it an hour later, three?*—Stu's nurse comes over and hugs me, saying, "I'm so sorry." And then another nurse comes over and squeezes my hand. *What is happening?*

Alan rushes to find the hospitalist, who has disappeared and then reappears, announcing, "I have ordered a helicopter to fly the patient to a crisis center. This hospital is no longer equipped for your husband's condition."

Words I have pushed away since 3 a.m. suddenly take over: that Stu could die—not in a vague sometime, but now. For years I've rehearsed "what if" scenarios, with every thud upstairs, every phone call when Stu travels alone. I never rehearsed what I say in panic to Alan now: "Maybe we should keep Dad here. Maybe we should just make him comfortable. Maybe you should call your sister." Julie is out west on vacation and mild pneumonia hadn't seemed worth calling about. Alan nods and we hug each other longer than we ever have, afraid to say more, afraid to weep.

I want to be with Stu, feel him close, but they've moved him to the other side of a glass window. We are being kept outside as four medics hover over him with pumps and tubes under harsh lights. Quick desperate moves that finally push me to ask: "What about hospice care?" The words feel like a betrayal and a gift. I know Stu wants no heroic measures when all hope is lost. But is that now? This hospitalist, this Dr. K., has offered only optimism, so how can he have Stu strapped on a stretcher about to fly away from me? There is no room left onboard.

"Hospice is not an option," says Dr. K. Two men are wheeling Stu through a doorway. "We have no beds or personnel for that."

"But my husband has a living will. It allows us to decide what to do. You saw it, read it." I try to sound in charge, the way Stu would be. People listen to him, but he can decide nothing now, so I, with his medical proxy, must make his choice.

The living will became void, says the hospitalist, when permission was given to treat pneumonia with IV antibiotics. A total misinterpretation, lawyers tell me later, but that was what led

Dr. K. to write, "Do everything!" on Stu's chart. And that's what the staff has been doing.

"My husband wasn't in crisis; there was no emergency. He just had mild pneumonia. You kept saying that." No matter. "But it's a legal contract." No matter. I feel the voiceless fury of a dream. Stu has wishes and rights to dignity without futile end-of-life measures. Listen to them. Talk to me. No one is paying attention. No one is telling us if his death might be happening or not.

Stu is flown by helicopter to the big hospital while I drive like mad up the interstate to get there first. Alan is at the house getting my toothbrush so that I can stay overnight and keep rubbing Stu's back. We have hope, you see. Even driving north on the highway, I don't really think death. What I think of is Stu in the helicopter and how he hates a wild ride when he isn't in charge. After his heart attack, he'd tell everyone: "I knew that *if* I survived the ambulance ride on the I-95 during rush hour, I'd live."

Dr. R. is waiting to take me to the Cardio Lab. They resuscitated Stu three times with cardioversion procedures, he says softly. "I wanted you to be able to say good-bye." I try, with growing dread, to be grateful. Young doctors and nurses file out of the lab, leaving Stu and me among the machines, huge and humming. I stroke his hair; he does not speak. I kiss him, talk to him, convincing myself that he can hear me say *I love you*. That it isn't too late, that he didn't die in the air, alone.

*****

"We were duped!" I tell my New Jersey internist a month later. She wants to know how I am, and I say that I'm trying to keep busy, not sit in dark rooms. Much of my grief has turned not to tears but to rage at my helplessness on that August day. "All those tests and procedures—and Stu was dead within twenty-four hours." I feel violated by greed and arrogance. The barrage of hospital bills fuels my cynicism even though I have good health insurance: IV antibiotics, aspirin, echocardiograms, two in-house cardiologists we never saw, and $18,000 for the helicopter that flew Stu north to the big hospital two hours before he died. Or maybe he was already dead. Maybe the little New England hospital didn't want Stu as a death statistic—and shipped him out.

My internist is a card-carrying member of Compassion and Choices (that's why I picked her), so I don't expect her challenge of my outrage: "If there is even a 30% chance of saving a patient, you have to take it," she says. "Especially when things are changing quickly as often happens with older people." She suspects septicemia as the cause of Stu's death. Septicemia—a word I look up online:

A sudden severe infection...life threatening for those with weakened immune systems... often caused in hospitals...

Did septicemia kill Stu? Dr. R. suspected it too, especially with Stu's immune system weakened by the emergency appendectomy three months earlier. Septicemia can move fast, especially in hospitals. Did he catch it there? I never found out because no one in the little hospital ever mentioned the word. Only pneumonia was mentioned as the cause of death.

What my internist—and every doctor I talk to—can't understand is why the hospitalist didn't call Dr. R., Stu's cardiologist up there. "*We* emphasize collaboration," my internist says.

A friend on Princeton Hospital's Ethics Board reinforces that idea: "Our hospitalists must contact the patient's doctor if at all possible."

"Perhaps in theory," I say, before telling him how my neighbor took her husband to our emergency room and the hospitalist in charge (yes, they are in New Jersey) refused to call the family doctor "because he doesn't have hospital privileges."

My bioethicist friend can't believe it, investigates, and gives me a call. "A bad apple," he says. "That doctor was dismissed soon after."

Most hospitalists, I hope, are good apples, because 42,000 now practice in American hospitals. We are all likely to find ourselves in their charge when we climb into a hospital bed. Why? The upside is that they are trained to coordinate hospital care and be more efficient. The downside, as Stu and I experienced, is that they don't know the patients, have no context, and rely heavily on records and tests. If we are lucky, the hospitalist will contact our regular doctor; but collaboration, though highly desirable, is not required.

*****

It's been three years now, and I've mostly come to terms with end-of-life issues being messier than Stu and I thought when we signed living wills. And more complicated. Yes, there is a disconnect between ideal and real-time decisions. Yes, people often change their minds at the end of life. And yes, when things happen quickly, as with Stu, it's harder to enforce a living will than when dying is slow and more predictably timed, the way it was for my mother, dying at home of cancer, under excellent hospice care.

But one truth remains uncomplicated for me: the right to know what the doctors and nurses know—in real time. How else, living will or not, can we know when mild pneumonia becomes septicemia, and death is no longer a long shot, but close at hand? I said yes to IV antibiotics, yes to oxygen, yes to a catheter—all Do Nots of the living will—because Stu was sick but not dying. He would get well, and IV antibiotics were supposed to speed his recovery better than antibiotic pills.

When did that change? Certainly before the nurses hugged me to say, "I'm so sorry." Was the hospitalist too afraid to tell me? Too arrogant? Too embarrassed? Too unpracticed in delivering bad news? Or did he really convince himself that our initial yes to

IV antibiotics voided the living will and his responsibility to honor it? I still don't know because I never filed a formal complaint, thinking, who would listen? I know no one there. I would write this instead, warning others: be aware.

Whatever that hospitalist's answer, I don't accept it. The only acceptable one is what Dr. Besser, a wonderful doctor and friend, says he tells dying patients and their families. Often more than once until families—sometimes angry, sometimes weeping, sometimes in denial—are able to hear his guidance:

> "When I know, or even think, that there's little hope, I bring family and patient together and say, 'Look, we can keep trying everything. Or we can make you as comfortable as possible so you can spend the precious time that's left quietly, together.'"

How I missed those words on Stu's last day. How I wanted someone with expertise and empathy to offer me options, make a recommendation, and then genuinely ask: "Should we make your husband comfortable or fly him to the big hospital?" I imagine myself saying, *Yes, yes. Make him comfortable*—but, of course, that's after Stu had died. On that day of fading hope, maybe I would have said, *Go quickly! Fly him there. Save him, do whatever it takes to keep him alive.* I don't know. I can't be sure.

But if it were today, the helicopter waiting, I would want to make that choice. And with the right doctor's help, one who accepts the fog of hope and hopelessness, I would have had enough time for holding hands and good whispers in the private quiet of letting go.

# *Poem Beginning in the Body and Ending in a Landscape*

*by Jonathan Weinert*

Partly wreckage
See

Left leg

Not going as the leg once went
Not light

The way the light once went

Before the light went dim
And a field grew out of the dimness

---

Snow lay on the field

Like a Gettysburg of mice
In white uniforms

White combat boots and their small
White rifles

Spent beside them

---

A blanket of mice
All down the hill

Then drifts of mice at the foot of the hill

Glared sharply in the darkness
Like a photo of the moon

In hard sunlight

And the tops of the campus trees
Iced over

Also glared

---

Partly wreckage
The arms not going

As the arms

Once went
Names no longer clinging to their things

Ascending like a scarf

Of gathered breaths
To hang a few feet in the air

Above the field

---

My boy
My self

I'm sorry that I

Had to leave you there
With snow all up your sleeves

And your snow pants soggy

And your left glove missing
And your buckle boots

That's the way the light goes out of the world

---

And if this poem were a dream
I'd see myself

Sledding downhill over mice

Mittened hands gripping
The wooden handles

Of my Flexible Flyer

My face directed downwards
Toward the drifts

My legs bent upwards

Boot soles pointed
Toward the sky

Starless over glowing earth

———

The boy's intention
Circulates at will

Through his limbs

Like water
Through a network of pipes

Which will one day rust

And stand empty
The boy's house

Stands empty

And the walls
At one another glare

———

In the kind of silence
That the voice of builders

Who arrive one Monday morning

To take the walls down
Cannot demolish

But which goes on beneath

The rip of saws and hammers
Curses shouts rough laughter

The boy's house tells its stories

Even after another house is raised
On its empty footprint

And another family moves in

---

The silence underneath the house
Goes on

And the darkness

Of that earlier time
Still looks in at the windows

That are no longer there

And the mice in the field
Go on being dead

And warm

Like a foot

Of April snow

---

There are deeper silences

Underneath the silence
Inaccessible

But not destroyed

The silence of the people
Who passed this way before

Like dark trees flowing together

Up a hill
And at the top of the hill

They reach long fingers

Sticky with pitch
Up into the low dark sky

To fasten jewels there

Like lights
Fixed to the rafters of an attic

---

Or maybe the boy sliding downhill

In the dark
Is dreaming me

I hope that's true

Because that would mean
The boy's alive

And not alone

And the world is dark
And for a moment safe

With the real wind pouring

Through the campus trees
My left hip hurts

And the instep of my left foot

Not going as the foot once went
But the boy

Sleds like water

Running over ice
And the mice glow softly in the field

He's coming downhill

The way that I remember him
Now that he's disappeared

# *Making Peace with Pepperoni*

## *A Muslim-American Perspective*

## *by Nadia Viswanath*

The tantalizing smell of pepperoni pizza. Greasy, cheesy, meaty, salty decadence—to me, it wafts of paradise. Once my go-to late-night snack in college, I have since given up pork.

I don't eat it anymore as a tribute to my mom. To you, that may seem strange, and my American sensibilities wholly acknowledge that. But to my Muslim sensibilities, other dynamics are at play.

My mom is a devout Muslim. Raised in India as one of eight, by two hard-working, equally devout Muslim parents, my mother's faith runs deep. She does not drink, prays daily, fasts in the holy month of Ramadan, and makes donations to educate poor children in India in the name of Allah.

She passed on these traditions to my brother and me. Growing up, an Arabic teacher came to our home each Sunday. We learned to read Arabic, the Quran, and the tenets of Islam.

Like many kids, I loathed my religious classes. I whined incessantly about Sister Munira's visits and complained that other kids didn't have to learn Arabic or read the Quran.

When I was fifteen, my mom departed from South Asian

tradition and obliged her American children in their free-willed natures. We were allowed to stop our lessons.

I'm not sure if I consciously stepped away from my faith, or if my never-ending list of homework assignments, tennis matches, and basketball practices carried me away by default. It was likely a convenient combination of the two.

Another factor complicating my relationship with Islam was that I was "half." My dad is Hindu, and in my tumultuous teen years, I let my two divergent identities guide me away from both religions.

In my early twenties, I found my way back. This time, I returned to the religion in a different way, reacquainting myself with Islam through a cultural lens rather than as a student of religious texts. I connected with Muslim friends, read about perceptions (and misperceptions) of Muslims in the media, and began to advocate for my faith.

I am not the same Muslim I was as a child. I don't read the Quran weekly, pray daily, or fast. I drink, and also find calm and centeredness in Hindu ritual prayers.

But I will not eat pork. Why? To honor my mother and her religion. It's my own quiet way of subverting all the forces around me that seek to diminish my Muslim-ness because it's easier to move through the world as an American, eating whatever I want, wearing whatever I want, and spending my time however I want.

My selective application of my Muslim faith leads to nearly weekly conversations that follow a similar trajectory:

*What is your background?*

I'm Muslim.

*[MOMENTARY SILENCE] Oh, I had no idea! But you drink?*

Yes, I do.

*[INCREDULITY] Do you fast?*

No, I did occasionally growing up, and my mom still does,

but I don't.

*Oh.*

What they really want to ask is: how can these truths live together?

Non-Muslims aren't the only ones who hold a narrow definition of Islam. Muslims, too, express the same confusion and disbelief at my claim to the religion. We apply a double standard to Islam versus other religions like Christianity, Judaism, and Hinduism. For other religions, we have come to accept a more fluid expression of religious identity. "I'm culturally Jewish," is a sentence I've heard countless times. If Christians don't go to church every Sunday, we aren't confused. But my selective application of my Muslim faith presents a sort of dissonance.

As young American Muslims, we must take control of defining our Muslim identities, rather than having others define Islam for us. By creating fluidity in the definition, we lessen the harsh rigidity that surrounds current perceptions of the faith. We build a wider tent of people who can identify with the multitudes of this beautiful religion. We can learn from other minority faiths like Judaism on how to better become a "more regular part of the American fabric."

Back to pork.

One lazy weekend this winter, popular television handed me a revelation about pork. Nestled into the tired sofa of my cozy Cambridge apartment with a steaming cup of mint tea, I indulged, for the millionth time, in reruns of *Sex and the City*. In Season Six, one of the main characters, Charlotte, converts to Judaism for her boyfriend Harry, a Jew who insists that he must marry a Jew. The season itself is a fascinating case study in how to explain a religion to a wider audience on popular television, but the first episode really hit me hard.

In the episode, Charlotte and her boyfriend, Harry, are out to dinner. Charlotte has just learned of Harry's requirement that he must marry a Jew, and is sussing out the religion. Harry orders the pork chop for dinner, and Charlotte balks. Harry prods her, and Charlotte explains her reaction, admitting, "I'm confused, I mean you can order pork but you can't get serious about a future with me because I'm not Jewish."

Harry responds, "Charlotte, it doesn't work that way. I'm not kosher, I'm Conservative."

Through the lens of a casual date night, *Sex and the City* reminded its substantial viewership that being Jewish doesn't equate to a rigid list of qualities, behaviors or limitations. Being Jewish can be defined fluidly, as a cultural expression or as a holiday-time reason for celebration.

I frequently play out a parallel scene in my mind. What if Harry were Muslim, and Charlotte were asking how he could order a glass of wine and still be Muslim? A scene like that would do wonders for Muslims in America, showing the many faces and expressions of Muslim faith.

Hollywood today does the opposite. Shows like *Homeland* and *24* further perpetuate a singular trope of Muslims as terrorists. *Friends*, one of the most-watched shows of all time with massive global influence, doesn't mention Muslims once in ten seasons. Even newer, more socially aware shows like *The Mindy Project* only occasionally mention Islam, and only when Mindy corrects people who think she is Muslim.

If television depicted Muslims with funny music and light storylines, rather than sinister music as a backdrop for terrorism, Islam might be viewed differently, as Aziz Ansari pointed out when he hosted *Saturday Night Live* in January 2017.

Indulge me, one final time, in a return to pork.

You are wondering why I don't take my own advice about defining my Muslim identity on my own terms. Why don't I just order a slice of pepperoni and satisfy my long-held cravings?

For me, giving up pork feels good. It is a small, quiet way that I honor my mother every day. I accept my no-pork pledge as my practice of my identity in the same way that I accept others who selectively apply their faiths or cultures.

My favorite verse of the Quran is called 'The Disbeliever' and it ends, "for you is your religion, and for me is my religion." So, for my Muslim brothers and sisters out there, I urge you to lay down your own parameters for your faith, and share that with others.

If you'd like me to pass you a slice of pepperoni, I gladly will—as long as you don't roll your eyes when I order myself a beer.

Published in conjunction with Harvard's Kennedy School Review

# *Microwave Oven*

## *by Mitchell Krockmalnik Grabois*

I once had a friend who was a microwave oven. She heated up quickly, but had a cold heart. I went to high school with her. We kept in touch over the years.

She married a man because she believed that as he aged, he would grow more and more to resemble his father, whom she greatly admired. But as he aged, he became the antithesis of his father. It made her bitter. Her glass door became greasy. You could no longer see what was inside her.

I talked to her on the phone. I was thinking about all the appliances that I've owned that have broken down and I've discarded.

I had a friend who was a vacuum cleaner. I had a friend who was a dishwasher. I had a friend who was a ceiling fan. My wife told me that all my friends are marginal, which was the way she reminded me of how marginal I am.

This friend, who was a microwave oven, aged. The hinges on her door weakened and she began to release dangerous radiation. At night I would imagine myself spinning on her carousel and would get excited and couldn't sleep. I put a cup of coffee in her and carelessly pushed some buttons. The coffee boiled over and seeped through the bottom of the door. It kept pouring out of her.

# *from The Sea Ranch*

## *by Jared Stanley*

My skin changes direction, migrates
to sleep. "Sleep" means "I tongue at my left eye
as it slowly descends into its socket
*from heaven as if by a chain*
'til my tongue won't reach."

Little honeybee sucking at the cup-shaped eternity:
The left eye has its unbuilt plan,
as if a city: Ecbatan
Xanadu
Cibola
Winnemucca
The looming of outskirts in starlight.

And *by* starlight, I touch cities projected
onto the eye's convex arrangement. I pry open
The lid a sliver; the roof gives way
To a cold and open dome, its sister sphere:
Both blink in the pinpricks of their names (eye and sky)
I lip their sibling sounds, moan a bit and toss, pull the sheet
Between my legs in Shangri-la.

In smooth pursuit of our rest
sleep has no singular attention:
but hey hey hey
neither of us
Has a song to guide
the other either

so who's to say or
suss or chant?
Lulla, lulla
Shafts of noctilucent gray
smack the brim of a leaking hat
*this means mentally reconstituting paradise*
But hey - now what?
Don't blink me to sleep.
Don't blink mean sleep?
Don't its blinking mean sleep?

Somehow we open
the heavy front door
And both fit through
while holding hands
awake-seeming, barefoot
but sleeping.

Four porcelain cups wait for us outside
in the mossy gravel.
It feels like a ritual
Gray light, damp.
Eight eyelids almost touch
many lashes shield the slits.

They're porcelain coffee cups like my grandma's,
decorated with North American songbirds
brims lined in real gold
the kind that spark in the microwave.

The cups like nothing else
the pelican, the hedge
muted but visible.
Blink go the lights on the opposite side of the bay,
the eyelid's visible memorial to waking.

We pluck out our eyes
place one in each cup
cup each with both hands
kneel as if putting an egg on the ground;
it seems the thing to do.
The eyes slide on a film of tears
Into the brim neatly
The cups like new skulls
as if the blood in our heads had been granted the right
to give off that rich dull color of gold seen by candlelight
though I don't know what you're thinking
while you yank on yours

plucked whole from some sockets,
Our eyes stick like jelly to the lip of the cup
and when spilt, like slugs to the soil.

Others are asleep in the next room.
Can they hear our breath
its dignified beat, almost a footfall
in this folie a deux
*when you and sleep escape me*?

# *Dismantling Communication —Literally*

## *by Maisie Wiltshire-Gordon*

A friend was telling me about a particularly awkward experience recently—which I will not share here, except to remind you that coffee is indeed a diuretic—when she happened to say, "I literally died of embarrassment."

It was hard not to offer a snarky reply. Literally died? What, exactly, was she asserting? "I was murdered by my own shame. And, on the third day, I rose again so as not to miss this coffee date."

I held my tongue: honestly, she had been through enough. Except, of course, a literal death. It would have been more truthful to say, "I *figuratively* died of embarrassment." Or, "It was *like* I died of embarrassment." But literally? She hadn't died. She'd *lied.*

And it's a dangerous thing, to say things that aren't true—even when no one is deceived. We expect certain behaviors of one another in conversation, and these shared assumptions enable effective communication. Paul Grice outlines these expectations with four maxims that linguists refer to as "the cooperative principle":

1. Quantity: Be as informative as required—not more or less.
2. Quality: Don't say things you believe to be false, or don't have any evidence to support.
3. Relation: Be relevant.
4. Manner: Be lucid, avoiding ambiguity and wordiness.

Communication breaks down if we do not follow these maxims most of the time. Consider Quantity. "I have one brother," I might say. And this is true—but I have another brother as well. If you couldn't count on me to follow the Maxim of Quantity, you'd have to check every assertion I made. Our conversations would become laborious and unpleasant.

Or say I'm going for a walk. My roommate, looking at the Paris weather report, announces, "It's raining." But (as I discover after donning my boots and raincoat) this is irrelevant to the walk I'm taking in Boston. If I can't count on my roommate to follow the Maxim of Relation, it becomes much more difficult for us to communicate. Grice's Maxims form a common foundation that allows us to interpret and understand one another. So by asserting—despite knowing it to be untrue—that she literally died, my friend deliberately chipped away at the Maxim of Quality.

Her use of "literally" violates the Maxim of Quantity as well. "I died of embarrassment," she could have said. Adding "literally" to her statement doesn't add any new information. The words she used already had their literal meaning. She's already said, literally, that she died of embarrassment.

So why say it? Why violate two maxims of communication, maxims that make it possible for us to understand each other? Our ability to communicate is at stake. Why risk it?

After all, thanks to the Cooperative Principle, we *do* manage to communicate successfully most of the time. The salami is in the refrigerator, and the cheetah is the fastest mammal: not much question there. We make certain assumptions, and usually it works out just fine. But usually—we say things people expect to hear, don't we? Maybe no one has said this *particular* sentence before. But for the most part, we're really talking about things that have already been talked about for years and years and years.

Some of it *is* new, of course, and that's where we run into trouble—trying to explain a new way to solve a problem, or a new way to look at the world. This is why literature is often so complicated: it gives us new ways of seeing. In his book *Principles of Art,* R.G. Collingwood describes literary expression as "like a gull over a ship's stern. Trying to fix the proper meaning [...] is like coaxing the gull to settle in the rigging." Literature is trying to say something new—which means we don't have words for it yet, although of course words are all we have to work with. We have to coax the gull to settle. Or, in the angstier promulgation of Eliot's J. Alfred Prufrock, "It is impossible to say just what I mean!"

When I first started studying poetry, I used to wonder: why do poets insist on obfuscating the thesis? But it is impossible to say just what I mean! There are no words for the thesis yet. Poets have to do tricky things with the words we already have in order to get at the things we've never talked about. The first jilted lover finally settled on the expression "broken-hearted" to help us understand her pain, and it worked well enough for a while—and still does work, in fact, if all you want to express is that your pain is the same as that of all the jilted lovers we've seen since then. (And let's be honest, it probably is.) But if you want us to think about this particular heart, this particular pain—we find ourselves back with Collingwood, coaxing a gull onto a rigging where it has never perched before.

When people use the word "literally" before a metaphor, it's tempting to respond: "You don't really mean that literally. You mean it figuratively." But the fact is, we *always* mean our words figuratively. There's nothing inherently salami-like about the word "salami". We connect word and object through our shared assumptions, our common uses, our convention that the word will be employed in particular ways. Every word begins as a metaphor. Rather than say, "I literally died of embarrassment," perhaps it would have been more truthful for my friend to say, "I was mortified." But is that so different, in the end? After all, the root of the word means "to put to death." It, too, carries the relic of figurative meaning.

"Literally" reminds us of the medium we use to communicate. No matter what we say, we will have said it literally, simply by virtue of speaking with words. But explicitly flagging speech as literal calls attention to a fact often overlooked: I used language to say this, and it is impossible to say just what I mean. Or, put another way, sometimes we mean something different from what our words mean. Saying "literally" reminds us that metaphor is an option, too.

We've become inured to most of the metaphors we encounter on a day-to-day basis. People admire the blanket of snow or lament a broken heart so often that we forget that these are metaphors. And in some sense, they aren't metaphors anymore. For most of us, "a broken heart" means roughly the same thing as "emotional distress caused by a loved one."

But saying "literally" breathes new life into the metaphor. It reminds us to look at what the words themselves are actually saying. "Broken-hearted" is a tired epithet. But "literally broken-hearted" is much more interesting. Of course the heart in question did not split apart. That was true of "broken-hearted" and it is still true of "literally broken-hearted." But "literally" says, listen to the words I'm using: I mean them! So we listen. And we think about what a literal broken heart might have in common with emotional distress. We imagine the pain in the chest and the feeling that the body cannot survive this way, rent in two.

Metaphor uses blatant untruth to pull us out of our everyday world. "But soft! What light from yonder window breaks?" Romeo asks. "It is the East, and Juliet is the sun!" Romeo has not gone insane when he says this. He's madly in love but he isn't *mad*. Nevertheless, in our world Juliet certainly is not the sun. Romeo is asking us to join him in another world, where she *is* the sun, to see how things look. Denis Donoghue writes about the "impulse in metaphor to escape from the world." We might add that, to do so, a metaphor-maker risks the very foundation of our communication. Language breaks down if we do not say true things most of the time. There must be something very important about Juliet that Romeo wants us to see, that he would stake on it communication itself.

There's a Calvin and Hobbes cartoon where Calvin's father is quietly reading his book. Calvin stands right next to him, inflates a balloon, and pops it. Of course his father is horribly startled. Calvin turns to him and says, "Pay attention to me."

That's what "literally" does. When I use a metaphor, don't just say, "That's nice, dear," and go about your normal life. Pay attention to me! There's something here I actually want you to think about! The word "literally" is my way of popping a balloon by your ear: listen to the words I'm using. Join me in the world I'm proposing.

We need common assumptions in order to communicate. We need to be able to count on each other for quantity, quality, relation, and manner, just as surely as we count on a common vocabulary as English speakers. Every violation of these conversational maxims diminishes the shared foundation that lets us communicate. Every time we say "literally" when "figuratively" would be closer to the truth, we disrupt those common assumptions. And for what? What do we gain by making it harder to understand each other? What is the value in rendering language unreliable?

In fact, language is already unreliable. We forget this amid ostensibly concrete expressions and metaphor that has long since turned to idiom. But "literally" reminds us: we can use words in many different ways; and we shape their meaning with every use. Thus "literally" awakens us to the power of the unreliable. This is how new things get said—through metaphor, through the uncommon use of common words, through the coaxing of the gull.

"I literally died of embarrassment," my friend said. It's not true, and such untruths could make everything come undone. But language is already undone. It's up to us to find new ways to tie it together.

# *Isle of Delights*

## *by Martin Chan*

The lake was alive with lights: the lanterns on the boats golden and round like hundreds of miniature suns, and the moon so heavy on the horizon it seemed impossible it would climb any higher in the sky. The foxes smiled debonairly as they steered the boats. They knew well how to mimic the behavior of aristocratic young men, though they couldn't entirely refrain from an occasional impatient yip, while their doll companions tried to wear the same demure expressions they had so often seen on their mistresses' faces.

How strange to find themselves on boats, the dolls thought. How strange to be separated from their devoted owners. One of them had been sleeping beneath a flowered coverlet when a fox leapt through the window and tore her from her protesting owner's arms. Another had been lying in a lacy crib before finding herself in a fox's mouth. It was all quite shocking, though the dolls weren't terribly upset. What young lady doesn't want to be abducted by a gay troubadour? The thought of their forsaken little girls was sad; nonetheless, the dolls couldn't help smiling furtively into their fans.

The Isle of Delights was in sight now, a black line in the glittering water. The foxes could barely contain their excitement, and the dolls tittered nervously. But wait, what was that along the shoreline? It almost looked as if there were broken dolls, thousands of them… One or two of the dolls screamed, but the foxes hastened to explain. You young ladies aren't accustomed to being out on the water, always all kinds of strange debris; you're seeing twigs and branches from the wind storm last week. The dolls tittered again, embarrassed by their ignorance, and the gallant foxes helped them ashore.

How glorious the night! It was the festival of the Mid-Autumn Moon, and the music of human celebrations drifted across the water, but even the humans weren't enjoying a repast as splendid as the one prepared by the foxes. Embroidered quilts were spread out on grass dotted with chrysanthemums sagely nodding their yellow heads. The dolls seated themselves and modestly pulled their silk dresses around their ankles. What would the foxes do next? Tiny doll hearts fluttered like hummingbirds.

The foxes, with a flourish, spread a bolt of golden silk over the embroidered quilts. The picnic hampers were unpacked, and what wonders they contained. Melons and mooncakes. Tiny jade cups, exactly suited for a doll's delicate hands, and wine as sweet as dew. Platters laden with red salted goose slices and pickled crabs. The dolls, accustomed to nothing more sumptuous than imaginary tea parties, were quite dazzled to be eating such splendid food, and perhaps they drank more wine than was wise, for a doll.

The foxes watched them carefully, whiskers twitching. Every fox knows that the secret to immortality lies in devouring a doll's heart essence, but opinions differ as to exactly what a doll's heart essence might be. The foxes had concluded on this particular Mid-Autumn Moon that perhaps a doll's heart essence was produced by feeding dolls pearls. After all, they had previously experimented with feeding dolls gold and orchids. Therefore, the platter they presented next was heaped with carp stuffed with nightingale wings and decorated with pearls arranged to represent a phoenix. The dolls exclaimed and applauded and daintily ate the carp, and the nightingale wings, and the pearls--every last one.

It was time. The foxes draped their front legs around the dolls' shoulders. "Look at the silver toad in the moon," they said. "Look at the Weaving Maid Star. At the Cowherd." The dolls lifted their little heads to look at the night sky and the foxes, with great delicacy, tore out their throats. Had they succeeded this time? The foxes looked at each other, hoping to see some indications of immortality, though they were no more certain what immortality looked like than they were certain what a doll's heart essence might be. But surely there should be some new luminosity in the air, a sparkle? They tore the dolls apart, searching. They didn't want to admit it, even to themselves, but this was ending like every other Mid-Autumn Moon night. Finally they climbed back in their boats and set off for shore, their lanterns long since doused. Even the human revels had ended, and the night was black and silent, the moon hiding behind a bank of thick cloud. A cold drizzle made the foxes shiver, and when they reached land they ran to their dens and curled up to shut out the freezing night, their tails over their eyes.

Winter arrived, and soon the Isle of Delights was muffled under heavy snow. The only movement was from the coiled dead leaves that still stubbornly rattled amid black branches. The dolls thought longingly of home and the little girls who had loved them, though they knew all that was past and gone. Their silk dresses, red as blood, blue as spring, lay in frozen heaps under the bare trees. By the time the snow melted the dresses were the same color as the surrounding mud. With the arrival of spring a creeping fungus turned the dolls' bright brown eyes to dull green. Arms and legs split open under the blazing summer sun.

But now it's once again glorious autumn. The night air is full of the sound of drums. The foxes are in their fairy boats, red coats gleaming in the light of lanterns. They reach the Isle of Delights, and their passengers cry out in fear when they see dolls dismembered and scattered about, but they are easily reassured. Soon a joyous party is underway. And why not celebrate? Perhaps this is the moon that will confer immortality. Perhaps this moon will bring each tender longing heart true love. Perhaps this is the Mid-Autumn Moon we have all been waiting for.

# *Fox Humana*

## *by Jim Krosschell*

If asked, the fox might say that one of the problems in her world, and ours, is that humans have overtaken her species as the most widely dispersed mammal. I might have asked her myself the other morning at dawn, but we were separated by the double-thick glass of French doors, and I was tongue-tied in awe. She didn't even seem nervous. She was on the deck, calmly probing the corner where the boards meet the house, interrogating the closed seasonal entrance to my shelter. I'm the kind of human who, when faced with emotion, freezes too soon and ripostes too late, and a more specific question occurred to me only later. I would have asked, "How do you live with us?"

I had watched her and her mate explore the front yard when I first got up. On most dark Maine December mornings, quiet of lobster boats and planes and chain saws, I'm in the habit of lying in bed and reading in the gathering light and looking southeastward over the bay until the red bump of sunrise climbs out of the sea. But that day I got up in the gloaming of morn, when mice and voles make one last run, when deer graze and foxes patrol, when humans are mostly peaceful. Drinking orange juice near the French doors, I saw first one gorgeous red creature, then another, come into the yard and make a few perfunctory sniffs, perhaps smelling my poodle's habitual morning toilet, then trot into the little copse of spruce to look for dessert or repose. Or so I thought. I had just started the coffee when I saw her again on the deck (I'm pretty sure she was female; they tend to be bigger than the males). She was clearly asking questions of the glass, the section of trim slightly rotting from salt air, the hulk of the house. Did she see the invader standing stock-still five feet away? Was I a harmless or a menacing shadow in the glass? I don't know. I have no idea what an animal thinks (except when I'm entranced by an animal, and then I'm not thinking at all). I do know that I didn't really need caffeine (or email or even Trollope) that morning. I was high on natural possibility.

The fox and many other "resident urban" carnivores and herbivores are thriving even as life for humans in our cities and suburbs becomes more dangerous. Deer and coyote and turkey and fox, formerly wild, now exist in a kind of half-tame state, still a little wary around the bipeds but making an excellent living among their constructs. Of course, animals are generally protected by law, and the laws seem to work, which cannot be said of many of our attempts at self-regulation (witness: greenhouse gases, rainforest protections…).

With our own sprawling over-population we bring along other problems. In the early 1800s, for example, English gentlemen brought the fox to Australia; it now overruns the place, and along with its favorite prey, the rabbit, is considered a serious pest (the feeling may be mutual), to be shot on sight. As for human invasions, well, what mountaintop or desert dune is still safe from truckers and trekkers and do-gooding improvers?

Fox and human invaded New England more or less together,

traveling across North America from Asia and setting up their dens and longhouses when the glaciers retreated some 12,000 years ago. For the next 11,500 years humans lived peaceably here, evolving with the warming climate and diversifying landscape, managing their several tribal territories sustainably. They killed animals, certainly, but only for food or clothing, taking what they needed and not what they craved. Then the white man came, and how incredibly quickly life has devolved. In just 500 years (a blink of God's eye), white men were killing foxes to protect fat chickens and tame cats or for mere sport, and red men were killing foxes to trade their pelts for European guns and rum. Yet the foxes survived, and are thriving, giving us not exactly warm greetings but a cool tolerance.

Indeed, they thrive in the midst of us, smartly and calmly (as often we don't). Reynard is even getting along with his sworn enemy and cousin the coyote. Our parks and our backyards are justly divided between them. Natural laws work. Human laws help. And this peace has little to do with my own obsession, the conservation and protection of land and the creatures of the wild. Nature can thrill in a mown front yard.

But there is little to check the human population. In natural settings, plants and animals are found with friends and enemies, and this long-worked-out ecology provides a check on unfettered population growth. Invasives, however, are often transported without their evolutionary context. Kudzu and green crabs carry no gifts of coexistence. And what evolutionary context will check humans? The fact that we're the only species that willingly seeds its own destruction? Even on the relatively stable coast of Maine, a hundred years from now we may well have burned the land and poisoned the air and polluted the sea so much as to seek shelter, like the fox, underground. And when we emerge, will foxes and coyotes and wolves and even feral poodles find us wandering sightless, thirsty and cancer-ridden, and at last give us our just deserts?

Maybe Antarctica will be a safe haven. It's the one continent on which foxes don't live, and that was true for humans, too, until the crazed polar adventurers of the early 20th century "conquered" it for God and country. Yet the last hundred years have been relatively kind to Antarctica. No one owns it; the inevitable territorial claims were resolved by the Antarctic Treaty System in 1961, which cooperation, like New England's old Wabanaki Confederation, seems to work. Antarctica is also protected by its vastness, its harsh climate, its miles-thick ice, its minuscule population. The only exploitation so far is purely scientific; mining and fishing and whaling and sealing are prohibited.

And it too may be doomed. Antarctica might represent our best cooperative instincts as humans, but the chemistry of the cold Southern Ocean is particularly susceptible to lethal acidification. Wildlife and fish, as in all other oceans, are being strangled and choked by marine debris; sunlight breaks down that garbage into deadly microplastics there too; and how long before Antarctic ice, 70% of the world's fresh water, becomes a brand name? I can imagine the muddy landscapes, the schemes, and the wars of the future. Humans will swarm there like the foxes of Australia. What will kill the glaciers first, mining or melting? And there will be no one to shoot the pests except themselves.

Okay. Enough. (This is what happens when you ask questions of foxes.) For now, I'm content to observe a wonder of nature, an animal smart enough to have found her place in a changing world. I'm glad she has a den to escape storms and heat and guns. I'm thankful I still have one, too—and that for just a moment, we took in clean air and the warm red blaze of sunrise together.

# *Coupling*

## *by Dana Crum*

Somewhere between a spring-like winter
and a winter-like spring,

I lost you, lost you even as you strolled
beside me. Over clams and calamari

at The Little Owl, over chicken kori kebabs
at Kismat, you concealed

the matter behind smiles, behind drinks.
And what was the matter?

That you had fucked half of Manhattan
and all of Queens. That your exes, in dark puffy coats,

circled your building like fat birds of prey, waiting
for me to leave to swoop down and feast.

What was the matter?
That only countless men,

with rough talons and piercing beaks,
could drag you back to what the first man

you knew subjected you to.
That no man, certainly not me,

could convince you of a different kind of coupling.
Dinner might as well have been my body—

not satisfied, you devoured strawberry crepes,
their guts smeared across your lips.

In bed I drank Macallan to sleep
but could not sleep, could only watch

as night blanched and passed out.
The day you left, you wore a black frock

and black, studded clogs, gliding
through the room like ever-moving night.

I have moved too, dragged
by the illness that drove me to you.

# *Monster Love*

## *by Lesley Bannatyne*

*You sign a liability waiver and pay your money–for the chance to walk down a hallway two feet wide and forty feet long, in darkness, alone. Part of it you have to crawl. Music plays: Peking opera filtered through ice cream truck. Flashes come of things worse than you'd imagine on your own: medieval gynecology, a toilet teeming with snakes. You don't know what's next, but you do know it's probably hungry.*

This haunted attraction, "Midsummer Nightmare," was created by Josh Randall and Kris Thor (Vortex Theater Company in New York City), one of the thousands of dark entertainments that erupt in late autumn. Monsters emerge at Halloween just as the light leaves us and the first blast of winter cold shoots down from Canada. The presence of monsters—for millennia and as of this moment—means a change is coming.

It's supposed to be good for us, this coming nose to nose with them. David Zald, of the Affective Neuroscience Laboratory at Vanderbilt, explains that we gain mastery of our emotions by having encounters that we know are only partially real. Trucking with Halloween pseudo-monsters is a way to exorcise the rage and terror that festers just below our skins. They help us rehearse for real fear.

Our monsters have always come from serious places. After the trauma of World War I, Americans went in droves to see the movies' new horribles: *Dracula* (1931), *Frankenstein* (1931), and *Freaks* (1932). The Wolfman—Hitler's totem animal was the wolf—was the WWII monster, mutants and aliens our post-atomic villains; vampires obsessed us during the AIDS epidemic, horrific man-monsters erupted after Vietnam, and a spate of violent beasts came forth after 9/11. Monsters are, psychologists say, our repressed "evil twins," or our collective nightmares. To deal with the monstrosity in our lives, we make the monster real, externalize it, animate it, and kill it to rob it of power.

> By the dim and yellow light of the moon…I beheld the wretch—the miserable monster whom I had created. He held up the curtain of the bed and his eyes, if eyes they may be called, were fixed on me. His jaws opened and he muttered some inarticulate sounds, while a grin wrinkled his cheeks.
>
> –Mary Shelley, *Frankenstein*

But here's where our current relationship with monsters takes a left turn. Rather than externalize and destroy, some of us emulate, want to *be* monsters, to get so far out of mainstream culture that no one can mistake us for being part of it. Lizardman (aka Erik Sprague), a body-based performance artist from Austin, has had green scales inked across his entire body. There are guys with subdermal spikes in their forearms, women who bifurcate their tongues. Stretch your earlobes, pierce your nipple, tattoo your face. Joining the fraternity of the monstrous becomes an ideological stand, a way of saying, "I'm *not* you, *not* that." Burn the bridge, lock the door, don't look back. You can guarantee you'll never work on Capitol Hill if you tattoo OBEY on your knuckles. To avoid being co-opted by commerce, to outrun the media or any of the million rivulets of mainstream culture—to stay true to your revolution, to keep alternative lifestyle *alternative*—you have to transcend the artful exterior and sink down through the skin to the blood. Mark yourself—flay, pierce, rip, decorate (mutilation as creative dissing of normalcy, the ultimate parody of plastic surgery-obsessed America?). Slide right into the frames of those comic books and horror movies, inked or painted like those beloved monsters, into a reality that feels right.

So, then, the worst fears of parents and psychiatrists have come true: EC comics, *Creature Features* TV movies on Sunday afternoons, and all those weird imaginings *did* damage the psyches of young kids. It was those kids—little Stephen King, George Lucas, Tim Burton, and Steven Spielberg (who terrorized his sister Nancy by cutting off her doll's head and serving it to her on a bed of lettuce)—who brought their love for the creepy into the art, film, music, and literature they produced as adults, which influenced the next generation, who grew up to create the latex masks, special effects, metal music, and gory props that kids today can't get enough of. (And of course the bar's been raised—blood-and-guts-wise—over the past decades. It takes a far more visceral monster to thrill a generation raised on "Hellraiser" than one growing up with, say, "Betty Boop's Halloween Party.") For anyone born after 1950, Halloween and monsters slid into our consciousness together. We fear them, we love them, and some of us want to be them. What does it say about us that this year's monster is the creepy clown?

> "I'm either tripping, or his daughter is a ghost. She has no reflection in the mirror. #TheHauntedElection," tweeted @Mister_Seattle

—"Social media thinks Mike Pence's daughter is a vampire"—New York Post, July 18, 2016

Bloodlust for upending the world order is cresting. Milwaukee Country Sheriff David Clarke, Jr., tweeted that it was "Pitchforks and torches time" to deal with corrupt government and bogus media. "Monster vote" is what Republican strategists call the allegedly large number of Trump voters who live under the radar and will descend on the polls come November. "Donald Trump Goes Full Rage-Monster on Hillary and Bill Clinton," reads the header on an October 9 Betsy Woodruff piece in thedailybeast. com. "Can the Monster Be Elected?" asks Michael Tomasky, in the *New York Review of Books*. Just last week, a CNN reporter described Trump "spitting fire" at a campaign rally in Florida, and Trump himself talks repeatedly about "draining the swamp." The monster, devouring, hungry—all mouth—is awake. We stand and watch, slack-jawed. We created this monster, but are repulsed when it lives.

Which is why Halloween comes just in time. Holidays put us on the same page—a truce, a cease fire in the culture wars—and this one, our sugar-fueled, exhibitionist, fantasy holiday, opens up the possibility of finding our better angels. On this one night, we stand together in a shared flight of imagination, agreeing that babies are peapods and our pets are superheroes, that we welcome men in high heels and women with Mario Brothers mustaches, pre-teens who look a worldly 20 and dads dressed like Marshmallow Peeps. Yes, of course there will be plenty of nasty woman Hillary and devil Donald, because irony is and always has been a huge part of Halloween. (Sales of presidential election year masks usually predict the winner: Bill Clinton outsold George H.W. Bush, George W. beat Al Gore. But the world's largest costumer, Rubie's, says that this year there's something else going on: Trump masks are flying out the door because people are buying them to make fun of and to support, and, for the first time, guys have to think about dressing up as a woman). At Halloween we can wrap our arms around the reality of the other 364 days and satirize, emulate, exorcize, and celebrate it. Levees break. Banks fail, jobs vanish, bombs explode. The joy of Halloween is not that it's dark and we revel in that; it's that Halloween can bring a bit of light and laughter into this darkness. Our one-time children's holiday turned blood-and-guts carnival may just be the right antidote for a myriad of ailments, a delightful gimme for any number of alt-cultures normally banished to the fringe. In so many ways, Halloween keeps us together.

Which may be why we hold on so tightly to Halloween. No matter how much we try to stretch it, Halloween happens only when the light casts a certain length of shadow and the temperature slides. The night is dug into the year like a marker. Leading up to Halloween: creativity, anticipation, possibility. After Halloween: reality. The sheer G-force of accelerating time makes us cling to something organically cyclical, to hold tight to this one night of benevolent exhibitionism and group glee before the bitter dissension of November politics hits.

Bring on the horror movie monsters and mad scientists, serial killers, adult-size tootsie rolls, and yes, even sexy exorcists. Let's fling open front doors and give candy to kids we don't know, watch horror burlesque artists twirl prosthetic eyeball pasties and ride around with witch-striped socks hanging from the trunks of our cars. It feels good to align yourself with all the creatures that gather on this night; there's a creativity and passion there. There's joy in living by a code, no matter how offbeat or temporary, and in celebrating with strangers. On Halloween, the connections between us become visible, like a giant web that stretches from haunted maze to office park to biker's club to your kids' cafeteria, where on Halloween, the lunch ladies wear horns.

# *Narcissus*

## *by Lauren Camp*

My father moved out of her house without warning
as daffodil stems were throwing off bells, as the bells

of the church down the street kept forgiving.
In his apartment downtown, he studied his boxes

for purging. Outside, the sun held what it was hiding.
The a/c lurched on. Down below, on the beast of the road

a number of silvery trucks exerted in the slow nudge
of mundane routines. My dad's lady friend called me.

Hundreds of miles away, I sat at my kitchen table
watching the pots and pans reflecting

the torn edge of dusk. Her voice scaled
and reverted with his familiar indications: the worship

of quarters, the strength of his appetite
for emotional errors. I may have laughed—

more like a pluck, an eventual falling
as I thought of the permanent space

he takes in my heart. Scabs over squandered zeroes.
That night, I was caught as she sobbed.

I was unmaking every way he closes a day.
Because I knew he would again claim her,

my mouth did not reply. For her sake,
I did not want to be right. I was certain

my father was reclined on his couch with his eyes
falling down at the corners. Because he cannot but flesh

love, cannot but mantle nerve, and never could force
right despite evidence, everything remains his

for the naming. On the 21st floor, the sharp wind
reckons his windows, but its grit and debris can't reach

him. Elevators move floor to floor without anyone
in them. Another useless awareness, and one we'll forgive.

# *Female Pattern Balding*

## *by Janice N. Harrington*

The pursuit of beauty comes to this. Selecting
a wig color that will best match your eyebrows.
Code gender as a form of hypertext. Insert
any parenthetical equation. Insert a goldfinch.
Improvise the feminine. Improvise woman.
Improvise the swinging pony tail
of a long-legged lass on a spring morn.

The last child on earth to ever taste honey
will be born in Haigler, Nebraska. Irate apiaries
sell beeswax on the internet. (Actually,
it is paraffin. Actually, it is melted crayon.)
When they cut open the belly of Martha
the passenger pigeon, they found the stingers
of ten thousand honeybees. Some women
replace the hair along their brow with hummingbird
wings. Others choreograph new follicles
from elevator music. A woman does the best she can.

That part about losing fifty percent of your body heat
through your scalp is not true. Dog hair sprinkled
around your cabbage will scare away whitetails.
In the deer beds, she found tufts of deer pelt and bones.
Naturalists now know that deer eat fledgling birds.
No one knows how many hummingbirds can be
found in the bellies of whitetail deer.

Dioscorides, the Greek physician, prescribed
onion to halt balding. Mash one onion
with honey and apply to the scalp before bed.
You will dream of tears and weeping. You will
wake with a wet pillow. Your tears will not
wash away the baldness, but practice
will make sorrow or loss easier to bear.

One kilogram of hair in South India goes for $250.
Merchants ship washed strands to America
in steel containers. In Omaha, a woman
wears the hair of a woman from Mysore.
The hair whispers Hindi love songs.
The American thinks she hears the wind or,
maybe, a hummingbird's wings.

# *G. Industries Airblown Inflatable Hunting Snowman*

## *Scott Challener*

How comforting to be attached
To a little pump humming up the bill.

Low-voltage, guy-wired,
Standing with a long gun.

Bloused in camo, staked, tethered,
Blown into the visible—

Awake but not alone.
How comforting to be

Eight-feet tall, fully extended.
Perfect gainly seams

Burbling against a quadrangle of sky.
Ut pictura!

But finally, in the unseasonably
Warm weather unseeable.

One continuous billowy fabric
Rippling without knowledge.

How comfortable not to think of anything
And think it twice, not to see

Anything and see it twice, not to go East
Of anything—the tracks, Eden, drone-shadow,

The Eastern Garbage Patch—and go there
Twice.

Lo, seasonless mind.
The vista of the landfill down the hill

That stands upon itself
Mounded, terraced, dozing like a burning hill

In perfect native effigy.
Lo, the fertilizer

In the garage, vacuum-sealed
Under a plastic shroud

Waiting to make the dead spots
Grow.

# *Tourniquet*

## *by Rosalie Davis*

The day after I passed my ninth-grade finals, I began a summer job at a country inn. The tips weren't great, but I liked the way the long, lace-edged apron over the housekeeping uniform made me look older. And I could practice my French; many of the tourists who passed through Bethlehem, New Hampshire in those days were Canadians following Route 302 from Vermont down to the Maine coast. My morning shift ended at two, but I wouldn't have minded extra hours, and not just for the money. As with other kids who lived out of town, my social outings were limited. When I got home I did chores.

If Daddy hadn't gotten hurt, I'm not sure what I would remember from that summer. I had made a new friend who lived next to a tennis court and was teaching me to play. A local Smith College alumna had noticed my report card and offered to show me the campus in the fall. I had discovered Loren Eiseley's writing and dreamed of revisiting my mother's western roots. I seemed to be starting, at last, to find my own way.

July 20, 1972, though, would leave a mark on our lives as

indelible as my father's limp. Although he walked again, after the injury he carried a cane and hobbled, a kind of rolling gait like a sailor on deck in a rough sea. Some people who only knew him as an old man assumed he had been wounded in the war; he had enlisted in the Army in January of 1942. But when such thoughts were shared aloud, Daddy was quick to correct them; he was a grateful non-combatant, stationed stateside during World War II and most of his twenty years' service.

More often, a visitor who saw our shingle mill might guess he'd gotten cut on that. It was easy to imagine a thousand ways the 19th-century machine could hurt you. Daddy was always splicing the belt, sharpening the saw, oiling and adjusting the gears and levers to keep it running smooth. Mounted in the iron belly of the two-and-a-half-ton behemoth was a huge steel blade, thirty-six inches across, which spun so fast you couldn't see its shark teeth as it sliced raw softwood into hundreds of neat shingles by the hour. To power the monster, Daddy ran a belt from the engine of his best tractor to the mill's driveshaft. Between the main saw and where the operator stood was a smaller, enclosed planer, exposed only through a slot just wide enough to insert a rough shingle to be trimmed. The big saw screeched as it consumed the sixteen-inch blocks of pine and white cedar my father fed it, but the hidden blade made a muffled, fluttering noise, like a giant shuffling its cards.

On his Franconia farm in the 1920s and 30s, my Grandfather Davis had owned a Lane Manufacturing mill just like it—possibly the same one. Growing up around such a dangerous machine my father respected its power, and he never got hurt on it. It would be a small, common saw that bit him; the mill actually became part of his recovery. Long after the workplace accident that nearly killed him, Daddy sometimes recalled that July day with a wry joke. He would tap his left knee with his cane and say he had been wounded in the "War on Poverty." His was a survivor's laugh.

Afterwards, people said how strong my mother was, how tough. No one thought of trauma counseling, and anyway how would she have found the time? She taught school all year, played the organ at church on Sundays, and worked summers. The three of us still at home were 14, 15, and 17; our big sisters were 22 and 24, trying to finish college and find good jobs. Mama was always driving somewhere for them, and this was long before I-93 was finished.

The fifth of his mother's ten children, my father was orphaned, or semi-orphaned if you prefer, at age 13; his mother died suddenly of pneumonia, and he was one of the younger children who would be farmed out. He worked his way through Franconia's Dow Academy as (what was then called) a ward of the state, I believe. His work ethic was ever his ace. He worked his way to Master Sergeant in the Army, promoted until his sleeve was filled with stripes. In 1963 he retired and returned to New Hampshire to find new work, mostly in the building trades. Eventually, the mill helped him make a living from the cordwood, lumber, and shingles he could take from our land on the Bethlehem Moraine. (A vein of glaciated boulders, gravel, and fine white sand ran through our place which once totaled more than fifty acres: twenty wooded, twenty wet, and the rest rocky old-farm clearings.)

Work clothes replaced his uniform. He could never have enough green twill shop coats, flannel shirts, corduroy coats, canvas coveralls or nail aprons, mostly bought at the Sears and Army/Navy stores over the Vermont line. From an Amish catalog he sent for wool overalls with red suspenders. In the diamond heart of January, these kept him warm cutting up a tree deep in the woods or standing by the mill. In summer he wore a chambray shirt and blue denim work pants or overalls, like James Agee wrote about in *Let Us Now Praise Famous Men*.

When I was in grade school, Daddy left the house about 6 a.m. and his Dodge pick-up truck turned in to the drive about the time the after-school bus dropped us off at the bridge. He would come in, set his black lunch pail on the kitchen table, and set to work at home. In a pinch he cooked supper, usually chowder, omelets, or an Army recipe called "Salmagundi" (don't ask). When I was old enough, I took my turn packing his two-sandwich lunch, except for the coffee, which my mother poured bubbling hot from an aluminum percolator into his stainless steel thermos by dawn's early light.

He cut wood for the fire, plowed the driveway in winter, scythed brush in summer, and was always improving the house. Many workaday smells remind me of him: wood smoke and linseed oil; pipe tobacco and two-cycle engine exhaust; wet mortar and lead solder; goldenrod and green hay; stove black, shoe polish, melted paraffin; the pink fungicide from the seed corn only he touched and then only with gloves.

If he brought home the bacon, put bread on the table, and kept the wolf from the door, he drove himself to enjoy life, too. We went downtown Friday nights (that was when the banks stayed open late so working people could cash their paychecks), visited our local Davis cousins whenever we could, and went to church most Sundays, and always on Christmas and Easter. Pine resin, the fragrance of the North Woods, clung to his wardrobe even when he was dressed up.

In winter when the snow was right and the moon was full, he would take us night sledding. He had cut a long toboggan run down our steepest hill and when we flew down it he would whoop; we just hung on to the belt of his storm coat and hoped to land safely at the bottom, where he taught us to turn sideways and ditch the sled before we hit the fence that marked the end of our property. In summer he'd take us to Forest Lake, but it seems like all that fun was before he got hurt, which became, somehow, part of our growing up.

By the time I started high school he worked longer hours than ever, building his own business. Besides doing tree work, he was taking on small residential projects, as well as the odd jobs he had long done for summer people and second-homers. My mother kept his accounts, and made sure the taxes were paid and the bills were sent out. Now you could set your watch by how he appeared for supper at five o'clock, when we were supposed to have it served, piping hot.

Summer always meant time with our Davis relatives, and 1972 looked especially promising, because Franconia was celebrating its 200th anniversary. My same-age cousin Wendy was up from Rhode Island and had been staying with us. It was nearly five o'clock when her mother came to pick her up; Aunt Ginny had hoped to see her brother Eddie, but the hour came and went without any sign of Daddy. We ate supper, changed into good clothes, and waited, ready to go to the first festivities in Franconia as soon as Daddy got home.

Six o'clock, and still no sign of Dad. Any minute it seemed the truck would turn into the drive or the phone would ring.

It was still light when my mother began to make phone calls, calling everyone she knew who might possibly have a clue as to where our father was. "Have you seen Eddie?" she would say into the black receiver on the wall by the window that looked out on the drive.

Between calls she would turn to us. "Where could he be?" she would ask. Did we think he had gone to Canada? People did sometimes. It was only seventy miles away.

Sunset, then dark. Still no Eddie. No news is not always good.

My mother stopped phoning and began pacing. She kept asking, "Where is your father? Where do you think he got to?"

We couldn't imagine. Except for the time we boiled honey over on her new Corningware stovetop, my father never asked us to keep secrets from our mother. We looked again and again at the clock above the telephone on the kitchen wall for an answer as it measured our dread.

Just past nine o'clock, my mother answered the phone—on the first ring. "Mrs. Ed Davis," she said. She wore a homemade flower-print dress with tiny white picket fences running diagonally between blue and red forget-me-nots. She stood still with her back to us, just listening.

I was sitting at the kitchen table, staring at its Formica surface, patterned with silvery ice cubes suspended in water. Bought new in Denver, it had gleaming yellow and chrome accents, and already seemed part of the golden past.

"No," I heard my mother say. "Do *you* know where Eddie is?"

A pause while she listened.

"Yes," she said. "Yes, of course I'm worried."

She hung up and again turned to us. "Isn't that strange?" she said. "That was the hospital, asking me if I know where Eddie is."

Ten minutes later, the hospital called again. "We have Eddie," they told her. She should come right away. He hadn't wanted to tell her he was hurt, they said, or they would have called sooner. He had wanted to wait until morning to call, but now he had lost a lot of blood. No one dared keep the news from her any longer.

She put the phone back in its cradle. "He's gotten hurt," she said. "He's lost a lot of blood. They said to come *now*." She gathered up her purse and car keys, and disappeared into the dark.

What was a lot of blood? I wondered. At such times, your thinking mind seems to need to keep its distance from your feeling one.

It seems strange now that the hospital didn't call and tell my mother what was going on. I should explain that my father had worked a couple of years as the hospital's maintenance manager, and he knew a lot of people there, which was partly how he had convinced them they shouldn't call his wife. Regardless of the lapse in communication, his friends took good care of him that night, and he survived.

About midnight, my mother got back from the hospital, and she stood in the yard for the longest time. I went out and asked her what she was doing. She was listening to the sound from the drive-in movie and watching the fireflies, she said. That was back when the old Midway Theatre out on the Whitefield Road ran double features. From our yard you could see the screen flickering through the half-mile of woods that separated us, and hear the music come up at the end. But what my mother was really listening for was the sound the world makes when it is going on without you.

When she finally came in, she told us more. Daddy had been cutting boards to fix a porch, somewhere over the County Line, a location that still sounds like a place in a Country & Western song. The guard on the six-inch hand-held power saw had failed and come off, somehow, in the indeterminate way accidents so often happen. But the blade kept working, had gone right ahead into his left thigh at a neat forty-five-degree angle, just above the knee. Where you would naturally press something toward you that was slipping away, Mama said. It had cut into muscle, artery, and even nicked bone. The wound was deep and serious, but it must have been relatively clean.

Daddy's luck had turned when a combat veteran in the house across the street had seen the accident or seen him stumble off the porch afterwards, holding his leg and bleeding. Over and over through the years we would hear how the unknown soldier had run over and with a towel rigged a tourniquet. I don't know that man's name today, but I should. I believe he had served in World War I, because he was much older than Daddy, who had just turned 50. For a long time, when Daddy told the story, he would stop talking after he said "tourniquet." He had blacked out that day, and I'm not sure he remembered the ambulance driving him to the hospital. Also, it was the end of the first part of his life, and he was still getting used to the idea.

People do strange things to keep their sanity. My mother went back out to the car that night to get a green plastic bag labeled "Personal Belongings." Daddy's keys were in it, plus the clothes he had been wearing when he got hurt.

The next morning, when I came downstairs to shower, I found the tub filled with red water, filling the small pine-paneled bathroom with a smell of rust, salt, iron—the smell of blood. Floating in the water with the ruined work pants were thousands of black specks, like black flies.

What's in the tub? I asked.

Lots of tiny, tiny little pieces, my mother said.

Shouldn't we let the water out? I asked.

She wasn't ready, she said. The pants needed to soak.

So, instead of taking a shower I took a bar of soap and a towel to the pond across the road. My mother was enough afraid of us drowning or being molested by a fisherman that if it had been an ordinary day she never would have allowed any of us to go there alone.

When I got back I saw her kneeling beside the tub, wringing out the fabric. She drained the bath and refilled it several more times until the water cleared and the pants were blue again. Then she hung them on the clothesline, as if one-legged work pants were nothing unusual. This was how she got through the day after, and the day after that too. The quotidian tasks steadied her, gave her a path to set her feet in. This was the first lesson.

My mother had not been a worrier. But no one could yet imagine how my father would get back on his feet, get back to work. His Air Force "retirement" was not half enough to cover the bills. (My parents called it "supplemental income.") Mama was working at the same inn I was, and for the rest of the summer I turned my pay envelope over to her; I've been told that should never have happened, but I was grateful there was a way I could help.

My first grade teacher, Edith Stevenson, and her husband Fred owned the Valley View Inn, about five miles away from home, west across Cherry Valley. Mrs. Stevenson had befriended my mother when we first moved to the North Country, and she had become like the grandmother I'd never known. Now I called her "Muffin" like her other friends did—at least when we were out of school. Without making me feel sorry for myself, Muffin understood. Some days she'd keep me on after my mother had clocked out and gone home. I might eat lunch in the kitchen with her and Fred; they were both excellent cooks. While she finished up her work, she would send me to play the piano in the sitting room, water the geraniums on the patio, or dangle my feet in the pool. Then she would drive me home.

Sometimes we went the long way, down overgrown Wilson Road. Narrow and unpaved, it meandered through small old farms and wooded tracts that hadn't been cut in a hundred years. When we passed her friend Chloe's house she would tell me what fun they had playing French card games on Saturday nights. Muffin taught me how to play "Mille Bournes" too. Other days we took Cherry Valley Road to avoid Long Hill and would stop at the prospect behind Lyster's Farm to look across to Mts. Washington, Jefferson, and Adams in the blue distance.

If the air of home was uncertain, with Muffin I could breathe. She made me look up, made me keep opening my eyes to the beauty that remained. It was like in first grade when she had written *Look* on the chalkboard. Then she was teaching me to read. Now she was trying to show me that life would go on.

It seemed like Daddy would never come home. When Mama took us to visit him, he would be on the east porch of the old hospital; she would bring paperwork and they would go over it. But towards the end of August he finally came back to us, pale and quiet. The first thing he did was change into a work shirt and a pair of khaki shorts that he could pull on over the full-length cast. After a few days of hobbling around on crutches, he grew restless and started up the mill. He wanted to "stay useful," he said. And the garage needed shingling.

The next week, we celebrated my parent's twenty-fifth anniversary with a homemade three-layer cake, decorated with roses of pressed white gumdrops and the so-called edible silver-coated decorations grocery stores used to sell. The crutches lean against the dining room wall in all the pictures, and my parents look a bit shell-shocked, but by then Daddy was getting better. He had begun putting weight on the leg, taking a few steps each day. It looked like he would walk again. Maybe he would smile again, too.

For a while it seemed like the worst was over, like we would regain the lost ground. But my mother knew things would never be the same—what might have gone into launching us into the world went into Daddy's recovery. She despaired at sending her three youngest to college. She wondered how the family would afford two vehicles, or finish the addition to the house. Summer trips were out of the question; relatives would have to visit us. Yet how could it have been otherwise? He had always been both our navigator and our North Star—the light and the way. His injury cast us adrift, and would make us vulnerable in ways we had never imagined.

The pressure to choose a vocation and find work intensified, but my parents were distracted. Our middle-class aspirations were falling through the safety net along with whatever had been saved for college. My mother signed my tenth-grade course selections that September without noticing that I had checked "Geometry Two" over the college prep "Section One." "Studio Art" was offered for the first time at Littleton High, which was wonderful, but I began to spend study halls making pottery and painting abstract series, avoiding other study in the language lab and library.

Things cascaded; the next year my nearest older sister left home right after high school to go to work. By the time I was taking SATs in the fall of my senior year she was barely 19 and already married, already expecting a baby. It was only natural my parents hadn't noticed my growing indifference to such milestones as college entrance exams. My scores were well below my PSATs.

But my mother had been following a story in *The Littleton Courier*. A summer resident of Bethlehem (Jason Somerville) had left our town's high school students a legacy to pursue higher education. Graduates of the class of 1975 like myself were among the first to benefit. If the scholarship hadn't landed at my feet, though, perhaps I would have become a nurse, like my father's youngest sisters Marge and Helen. They weren't letting me give up on myself. Without this support, my world might have shrunk to the fabric counter at Woolworth's, my mother was so overwhelmed. She had begun to say "no" to anything involving new ambition, outside influences, or travel further than Burlington; Lake Champlain had become the new "West Coast."

The garden that was so emblematic of our house and land grew smaller too. That was the last year we planted all three fields, and the first year we did not get all the potatoes dug. Relatives visited. One of Daddy's lodge brothers (Alistair MacBain) mowed the lawn every other week. Church ladies helped my mother make pickles and jam and put up the garden. My mother's family probably sent money. Summer had always been a time to sew, but not that summer. My father's Rhode Island sisters brought us school clothes.

The cast stayed on past Labor Day, and became mottled in gold, bronze, and purple—bruise colors. When it finally came off my mother checked the long scar more than necessary. Sometimes, she would run her finger along it and say, "Eddie. Oh Eddie."

My parents lived another thirty years. Through that time the shingle mill provided him with steady work. It was a one-man operation, except when Daddy fell behind with a big order, and then we would help him spread the shingles out to dry on the sandbank behind the mill. The fresh cut shingles smelled wonderful, like Christmas trees, with the resin oozing up like beads of dew along the bark edge. They dried to a light gold and then whoever could would pitch in and turn them to dry on the other side before carting them back to the mill to be bundled, which was rainy day, indoor work. Wing Road shingles were first-rate, with the weather edge clear of all knots and flaws, and in demand for as long as my father made them. They kept him useful.

As Christians, we were brought up to privilege the spiritual over the material, but the things people leave behind can haunt you just the same. After my parents passed away, and I was sorting out a closet, I found something that brought me back to that summer day Daddy got hurt.

I recognized the gray-painted box. Heavy for its size, it was made of hard southern pine and lined in lead; it was designed to hold ammunition. You locked it down by tightening two wing nuts on long bolts, the way you close an old-fashioned racket press. The only ammunition my father owned were blanks for a parade rifle, but we used the chest, a relic from his 1942 basic training, the way other families used a safe. For a while we stored matches, candles, and batteries in it; I suppose it might have come in handy in a power outage or the atomic catastrophe we lived in such fear of. Everything would be lit up, we'd been told. I remember as a child being wakened by thunder and lightning, certain that the big bomb had finally dropped and the world was coming to an end.

Curious now, I spun the wing nuts off and lifted the lid. I shouldn't have been surprised to find it filled with cloth; my parents saved all kinds for mending. As I lifted out layer after layer of blue chambray, red flannel, olive Army wool, and khaki twill, I thought of the Bible verse, "do not sew new cloth to old," a favorite of my mother's when she was figuring out how to patch a garment.

At the bottom of the box, I came to the clean work pants, neatly folded, and faded to that inimitable pale indigo only denim acquires, with the triple-stitches of the felled seams still gleaming gold-brown. Thirty-four by thirty-two, Dad's size. The left leg had been shredded off above the knee. The pants had not been further altered nor used for mending. How unlike Mama to have kept something neither useful nor beautiful. Still so potent, so able to return me to that morning when she had knelt by the tub wringing out the blue denim in the red water, the fabric told part of her story. Like a canceled check or an old deed, it spoke to what she had lived through.

I wished I hadn't found it, hadn't seen it, hadn't touched it. Why did the mutilated cloth frighten me? Because it reminded me of what we can only learn from experience? Maybe worse, I think it reminded me that we are always at the mercy of chance. The fact that my mother had saved the pants has since convinced me that she too was injured that day, and that her recovery was less complete than my father's.

Though my mother had saved the cloth forever, I wanted to be rid of it immediately. What the hell! We burned quite a few things that summer, and as soon as I had the chance I threw the pants in the fire.

# *Siluetas / Silhouettes*

## *by Carol Dine*

*after Ana Mendieta*

i.
I'll return in blood-paint.
Santa Muerte, goddess of death,
my body imprinted
on a sheet
in a fissured portal,
Candlewood branches
arcing at my feet.

ii.
My art, my sex
enraged him.
He shoved me
through the window glass;
I spilled across Manhattan.

iii.
Beside the ocean
my open hands, vermilion
mark the sand ridge.
The tide comes,
washes the rest of my body
clean.

# *Talking Moharrém Blues*

## *by Margaret Kahn*

On his first visit from the town to the village, Matt's heart sank. The room he was supposed to teach in had no windows and barely even a door. It was nothing but a hovel, fashioned out of dried mud. But he put the best face on it that he could as he sat in the headman's house, sucking on sugar lumps to sweeten the bitter tea.

Ken, the regional director at the Peace Corps office in Tehran, had said they were sending him to a village with a spanking new school. When Matt complained to the other expats in town they told him it was par for the course. Nothing worked the way it was supposed to here. Iran is a very farce-y country, the more jaded ones liked to pun.

But Matt hadn't joined the Peace Corps to accept the status quo. The other Americans—army personnel, mainly, or businessmen intent on cashing in on the oil wealth--argued that Iranians were not ready for democracy, but Matt felt that everyone deserved a fair shake.

The first time he saw "his boys" as he came to call them, he wondered for a moment if he'd been assigned a special ed class. Ranging in age from about eight to eighteen, their heads were shaved and most of them refused to even meet his eyes. Instruction got off to a slow start.

English was the subject he was supposed to teach, but these peasant boys showed no aptitude for learning it. He cast about for ways to make it easier and tried teaching "Old MacDonald Had a Farm." As he led them through the verses and compared these peasants to an American farmer who owned his own land, he quickly realized how ridiculous this was. In college Matt had been a political science major. He had even risked riling up the censors here by bringing his most treasured books -- by W.E.B. Dubois, Franz Fanon, and Herbert Marcuse.

On the third day he brought in a song from another one of his heroes – the folk singer Pete Seeger. "Talking Union Blues" had come from his earliest childhood. He had literally learned it on his father's knee. His students leaned forward, their eyes rapt as he intoned the lyrics. He felt some relief in just saying the words. "Now, if you want higher wages let me tell you what to do/You got to talk to the workers in the shop with you./ You got to build you a union, got to make it strong,/But if you all stick together, boys, it won't be long."

As he chanted on he thought of the workers he had seen here. Men in the meagerest of clothes, barefoot some of them, throwing bricks to one another as they stood on rickety scaffolds.

Afterwards, Ameer, by far the best student, had taken him aside. "We do not sing such songs in my country," he told Matt a stern look.

When Matt confided to a couple of the expats what he had done they regarded him with amazement.

"What are you trying to do?" one of them asked. "Get your students thrown into prison?"

He felt ashamed then for not having realized where the real risk for speaking his mind lay. Not for himself, a protected American, but for locals listening to his dangerous talk.

But the damage was already done. He went from having 30 students, to five, and finally to none. He thought of calling the Peace Corps director in Tehran for advice, but then decided it would be stupid to admit such a mistake. Better to take a little break and hope it would all blow over.

By the third day he was tired of hiding in his house so shortly after noon he jumped on his motorcycle and headed out of town in the opposite direction from the village. The bike had been his one luxury, bought from a German tourist shortly after his arrival. He gunned the motor over dried-up stream beds, passing springs with tell-tale patches of green surrounding them. Under the wide blue desert sky, staring at the soaring mountains that ringed the plain, he started to feel like himself again.

The next morning the warm winter sun was already slanting in through the crudely glazed window when he heard voices outside followed by the creak of the gate opening into the courtyard. Through the window he saw a boy coming up the path, the chadored figure of the landlady beside him.

"The foreigner is in there," he heard her saying in her hoarse voice.

Matt wondered who exactly she was letting in. A passing salesman? The Iranian equivalent of the Jehovah's Witnesses? Or maybe it was SAVAK, the Shah's secret police, come to ask the foreigner what he was doing here. Although why they would do that was anyone's guess. He'd recently come to understand that everyone in this country just assumed all Peace Corps volunteers were CIA agents.

He pulled his pants on over his pajamas and went to the door. The boy with shorn head who stood there looked strangely out of context. The town was full of modern appliances, European cars, fashions from Paris. This boy with his baggy trousers and shaved head was either from the poor neighborhood near the bazaar or from one of the surrounding villages.

He must be selling something, Matt decided, when he saw the red plastic bowl in his hands. People hawked things in the alley all the time – mainly kerosene oil, but sometimes fruit.

"Mr. Mattoo," he said in heavily accented English. "Why you not come to teach us?"

Only then did Matt realize that this was Ameer, with his head newly shaven, probably for lice.

"I was feeling sick," Matt lied.

Ameer gave a solemn nod. "God willing you will feel better soon."

"God willing," Matt echoed. "*Be farmayeed.*" He gestured for the boy to enter his room.

But no amount of inviting would bring Ameer past the threshold. Instead he handed the red bowl to Matt. It appeared to be full of sour-cream-like yogurt. In addition there was a little bouquet of fresh mint, tied with a blade of grass. Matt stood in the doorway watching for a long time after Ameer went away, carefully closing the crudely hewn gate behind him.

After that, Matt never missed another day. He went to that dark hovel of a classroom – so hot in the summer and now freezing in the winter-- and taught them anything he thought might be useful – English, simple arithmetic, how to read maps. He wrote to a friend in the United States and asked him to send a kit he'd had in his own childhood. Called a "Visible V-8" it was intended for Americans interested in working on car motors. Matt thought mechanical skills might prove more useful than learning English. The boys in his school were not likely to ever attend college. The books alone would cost too much, not to mention the loss of their labor. Their families were serfs for the local landlord. Most likely their futures, if they didn't stay where they were, eking a living off the land, lay in joining the army.

The fact that most of the engines here weren't V-8's didn't occur to him until he was facing the customs officers and sweating over whether they would let him receive the package. Once they saw the plastic and realized it was what they called a toy they saw no need to confiscate it. Still, impressed by the shiny packaging, they forced him to pay double its price in duties. Hopefully, he thought, it would at least be useful for them to learn the vocabulary items – pistons, cylinders, crankshafts – that were probably borrowed into Farsi.

He swallowed his complaints and took the now-opened box filled with plastic pieces back in a taxi. He hadn't wanted to compromise it by putting it on the back of his bike.

As soon as he got it to his room, he wanted to take it out to the village. Only then did he realize that it was already getting dark. Night was not the right time to arrive with a bunch of little pieces of plastic in a place with no electric lights.

Reluctantly he waited until the following morning. It was winter now, but he woke most mornings with the sun in his eyes. It was warm on his back too when he went outside. Just as he was wheeling the bike to the gate, Ameer hurried up the alley, on foot and out of breath.

"Mr. Qorbanipoor says you must come right away. Important visitors are expected."

Matt hesitated. Qorbanipoor's title was agricultural agent. But Matt had never seen him show the slightest interest in crops. He inhabited an office in town where he fielded calls that always ended in him shouting, "Qorbanet" into the receiver, literally, "I am your sacrifice," presumably to the people to whom he owed his position. Qurbanipoor was not his real name, but Matt enjoyed calling him that. "Son of sacrifice" seemed about right for a man who was ready to sacrifice nothing for the greater good, like so many of the people put in charge of things here.

Now Ameer was telling Matt how it was finally going to happen – what they had all been waiting for. The village would get the school that had been promised. They were going to break ground for the building today.

Ameer hung on behind as they sped past the fallow fields. Matt noticed once again, how the sun made this ancient used up land, so full of erosion and cracks, seem fascinating. He loved the weather here. One or two brief thunderstorms were the only breaks in a series of days that were framed in turquoise and azure.

Ameer hopped off before they came within sight of the village. Matt got off his motorcycle alone. There were more people hanging about than usual. Children with dirt-streaked faces crowded around the motorcycle. It never got old. The arrival of the Peace Corps volunteer to their village was like the arrival of the afternoon bus. It gave them something to mark their days, something to look forward to. He smiled and waved the way he always did, and then he walked to the house of the village headman.

The men stood when he entered. The villagers had gaunt sunburnt faces and rusty black suits. The city men had paler skin and European worsted over thicker waists. After everyone sat down, the headman's daughter set a glass of tea on the rug in front of him.

After the ritual greetings, no one said anything. But Matt could see from the way their eyes met – past him, over him, around him – that before he came, they'd had plenty to talk about.

He kept stealing glances at his watch. Already these visitors were over two hours late. They were coming from Tabriz, to the north. It was part of a tour, a jaunt through the unwashed countryside. The royals, in the person of the Shah's mother-in-law, were engineering a series of photo-ops to show Americans and the rest of the world how much they were helping poor villagers. This was part of the Shah's so-called "White Revolution," where not only was the land supposed to be redistributed, the serfs were supposed to be re-educated. They might believe this in Washington, but Matt knew better.

Already he was starting to feel compromised by his presence, as if he were lending even more American imprimatur to what was going on. Whether the school got built or not was not the point. The point was that this whole thing was a sham. He was not a real teacher, just a Peace Corps volunteer. As for the building itself, how many times had he seen government construction materials siphoned off from their supposed recipients?

But of course he could say nothing about this. All he could do was sit and smile and look appropriately Western. Ameer had disappeared. But other students were there, Hassan and Bahman giving Matt embarrassed grins. Matt thought of the Visible V-8 back in town and wished he had brought it.

He was on his fourth glass of tea when his thoughts began to race. Why was he just sitting here? Why didn't he just call his boys together and take them away to the spot where he usually taught them? Or better still, organize. Have a real demonstration. The village didn't need just the school that had been promised years ago. It needed medical care, clean water, electricity.

Matt looked around him. A dung-fueled fire rose from the courtyard where the women lived, the so-called "harem." Probably they had been setting things aside for days, even months, for the feast they were preparing. The chickens that had to be killed, the pickled vegetables opened, the bread baked in the underground ovens. Matt sat in the lone folding metal chair the headman owned and thought of how the villagers would go without for months in order to impress the people they regarded as their betters.

Finally, three hours after the visitors were expected, a puff of dust rose down near the entrance to the village. No one had eaten for hours. It would have been impolite to eat before the visitors arrived.

The car came on slowly. A Land Rover, of course. The children, even the dogs, stood aside respectfully. As soon as it stopped, the driver jumped out and went around to pull open the door. A woman wearing a coat made out of some very rare animal stepped out into the sunlight.

"Welcome, welcome, we are your sacrifice." Mr. Qorbanipoor and his cronies moved forward as one body. Only Matt hung back.

Mr. Qorbanipoor had his arm outstretched. For a split second Matt imagined he had taken the hand of the woman in the leopard skin coat and kissed it and pressed it to his forehead the way the villagers sometimes did with their overlords.

But then he realized they were just shaking hands.

"I want to present Mattoo Summerson," Mr. Qorbanipoor said. "He is doing very good work here."

The woman in the leopard skin coat actually took a few steps toward him. Matt stood up. But then he looked down and saw that her shoes were high heeled with open work at the toes. The caffeine coursing through his blood coupled with his hunger made it all suddenly feel intolerable.

He wanted to ask if she had ever visited a village before today. If she had any idea of how the people here lived. Anger welled up in him. Anger at the way "his boys" had been treated. He felt the eyes of the villagers on him. Was he too going to be part of this charade?

But he couldn't say any of this. Instinctively he knew that if he spoke in such a way to a member of the imperial family that would be beyond the pale. So he did the next best thing – he backed away.

Everything blurred after that. He had no memory even of

anyone looking at him. He didn't see his motorcycle until he was almost on top of it. But once he was on and bouncing down the road, he knew he had done something unforgivable. This place was all about status, and power. No one even went through a doorway before determining the correct order of who should go first.

Still they took their time. The call from Peace Corps central canceling his position came six days later. Matt had not gone back to the village. Instead he had holed up in his room reading Solzhenitsyn's *The First Circle*.

He'd wanted to be a dissident but all he felt like was a failure. Now he would never be able to help anyone here. For a few moments he allowed himself to wallow in regret and self-recrimination. Then he pulled himself together and started throwing books into a suitcase.

Later in the day he was nearly finished with packing when a knock sounded on his door.

He pulled it open. Ameer stood there, empty-handed this time.

"May I come in?" he asked.

Matt shrugged and went back to his packing. It was the height of rudeness, at least in this place, not to offer words of welcome or tea

But if Ameer felt insulted, he didn't show it. "Can I help you?" he asked, entering without being invited.

"No thanks," Matt told him.

Still he didn't leave. "You will take the plane?"

"Train," Matt said.

After Ken's call Matt had debated with himself. He might have flown if the Peace Corps Director hadn't been so insistent that he avoid Ashura.

This was the name of the upcoming "holiday" if that's what it could be called. So many of the sacred days on the Muslim Iranian calendar were to honor martyrs. The other expats had warned him about it.

"Everyone takes to the streets," they said. "It's weird stuff."

Clearly Ken thought so too, and urged Matt to take the plane. But the expulsion order had only fanned the flames of Matt's contrariness.

"I am coming with you." Ameer said in a way that was not a question.

Matt stared at him. The thought crossed his mind that he might be working for SAVAK, assigned to make sure the disgraced foreigner actually left. Why else was he here? Matt didn't understand it.

"Ashura is day after tomorrow," Ameer reminded him.

"Yes, I know," Matt said.

"My father's brother lives in Tehran. You will be our guest."

Matt studied him and then shrugged again. What did he care? The Visible V-8 was already in the hands of the trash man, who had accepted the box joyfully and then stopped at the end of the alley to puzzle over the contents.

The next day the train station was jammed when Matt and Ameer alighted from their taxi, struggling with Matt's luggage. Matt started having second thoughts when he found out there was only second class available and they wouldn't have their own compartment. But it was too late. Flights out of town were all booked. Ameer grabbed his heaviest bag and they climbed up into the car. Walking down the corridor Matt stared at the vintage wood paneling and oval shaped windows facing into the compartments. Some of them were already being draped with the dark fabric of chadors.

When they reached their own compartment, there were no veils, and no women either.

"Excuse us," he heard Ameer telling everyone. "This is my

teacher. He needs a place to put his books. He has many, many books."

The two of them pushed hard to get the suitcase into the luggage rack above the facing leather seats. Then the train started up.

"Where are you from?" a man wearing a tight fitting turtleneck under a shabby suit jacket asked.

"Canada," Matt said before Ameer could pre-empt him.

"What are you doing here?"

"Studying poetry," Matt told them in Persian.

Their jaws dropped, as if by not hearing the expected replies they had no idea how to go on with the usual barrage – how much do you make? Are you married? Why not?

Later, when he and Ameer had gone to the dining car, Ameer asked why he hadn't told the truth.

"It was the truth. I was born in Canada, and I love reading poetry, especially Rumi," Matt told him.

If Ameer was surprised, he didn't say so. Not until he had finished sucking the bones of the *jujeh* kebab Matt had ordered. These he pronounced not very fresh.

Matt felt a little thrill at such rudeness.

"Would you have preferred the dry cheese and bread that man was offering back in the compartment?"

"Don't worry," his student said. "The food at my father's brother's house will be like the food in paradise."

Walking back through the long swaying corridor behind Ameer Matt felt off-balance in more ways than one. He still had no idea why Ameer had insisted on coming with him. Still less why he wanted to introduce him to his family.

Back in the compartment, mellowed out from the meal, Matt studied the others. The man in the turtleneck eyed him back curiously. He had a *zoorkhaneh* body. Matt had only heard of these "houses of strength." He'd never had the chance to visit one of the traditional all-male gymnasiums.

"American?" the man in the turtleneck was inquiring in English as if he didn't remember Matt's previous answer.

Matt sighed and then nodded.

"How long you here?"

Matt cocked his head noncommittally, as if he didn't quite understand. He could see the man working hard to think of more words in English. But after a few seconds he gave up, and began talking to Ameer.

Matt listened as Ameer explained how Matt was his teacher and that he was accompanying him on a mission to Tehran.

"Why are you helping him?" the man asked.

Ameer shrugged. "The principal of the school has asked me."

Matt looked away, tired of trying to unravel why people said the things they did here. After awhile he closed his eyes. He was starting to think again about how his father would view this expulsion order.

In his younger days his father had been something of a firebrand too. Fighting for the rights of unions as a labor lawyer. But then unaccountably, he had switched sides. Matt wasn't sure of all the reasons behind it. The obvious one, which his parents had already told him, was that Matt's grandfather had died and his father needed to take over the family firm.

"They specialized in corporate law," his mother had told him. "It was a wonderful practice. It made us a good living. You shouldn't judge him too hard."

Matt could barely remember that firebrand father, the father of "Talking Union." The version he had now had wanted him to go to law school instead of joining the Peace Corps.

Matt had never bothered to write his parents about the real situation here. So there was no way to explain about getting kicked out either. Yesterday he had sent them a cable saying he would be arriving home shortly. He had no idea what reception awaited him.

The compartment had gone silent. Matt opened his eyes. They were all watching him. His heart pounded. He had heard the stories Americans told about the things that happened to foreigners here. Three years earlier, an American in a neighboring town had had his throat cut on New Year's Eve. The expats presumed the man was gay, which Matt wasn't. Still. What if someone just thought you were gay?

"They want to know if you like our music." Ameer was suddenly translating.

Matt looked at the faces turned toward him. "Yes," he said simply.

Ameer started to translate but the the man in the turtleneck was already smiling and saying something back which Matt didn't understand.

Ameer translated, "He wants to sing a song for you."

Matt thought of his experience with "Old MacDonald." None of his students had ever volunteered to teach him any songs although he'd asked them.

"Sure," he said now. "Tell the man I would love to hear his song."

The man in the turtleneck spoke again. "It's a sad song, in honor of Hossein's martyrdom. For Moharrém"

Ameer nodded, but he didn't translate.

The song began. The first part was almost like an exercise, a warming up. Matt listened, thinking at first that it was nothing special. But then it grew on him as the clacking of the train wheels faded. The man had an incredible tenor voice, full of richness and vibrato. Matt closed his eyes, feeling his body soften as the music flowed through him. If only, if only, the music seemed to say. If only

Hossein had not been slaughtered that day on the plain of Kerbala. If only the righteous had remained in charge of the caliphate.

Matt thought back to the historical overview the Peace Corps had given him. In the early years of Islam, the Arabs had conquered Persia. But Iranians in a sense had never really been conquered. The religion the Arabs brought had spectacularly fractured on the nearby plain of Kerbala where a group of men had brutally murdered Hossein, the heir apparent to the caliphate. Since then Islam had had two warring factions – the Sunni and the Shi'a.

It had all happened in the lunar month of Moharrem, the name given to the "holiday" they were now "celebrating." The *ashura* or tenth day, was what Ken had warned him about. That was the day Hossein had been murdered.

The song had ended. Once again Ameer translated. "He wants to know if you liked it."

Matt looked at the pairs of eyes trained on him. For a second he started, feeling that they'd seen his vulnerability. But then he realized that what he was feeling, they felt also.

"Yes," he heard himself say. "I liked it."

There was another moment of silence. Then the spell was broken as they began pulling the seats out and sliding the backs down until it was like one big bed, covered in aging leather. They stretched out gingerly, draping their jackets over them. Matt lay between Ameer and the window.

Even before the dawn light cracked in beneath the shades he could hear people out in the corridor, lining up for the lavatory. Ameer was still sleeping. Crumpled like a child under the cheap imitation American windbreaker he wore.

Matt lay still as long as he could, willing himself back into the sleep induced by the rocking of the train and the singing of the song. He was too tired to get up. Too tired to do all he needed to do before leaving this country. But it was too late. The day had begun.

He edged out into the corridor, feeling conspicuous. But no one seemed to notice him. They were too intent on getting their turn in the filthy toilet. When he came back to the compartment, without speaking he and Ameer gathered their things together. The train was pulling into the suburbs now, clacking past houses with bits of mirrors and colored glass stuck into their concrete facades.

In the big south Tehran station, the platform was thronged. But the mood had changed from the day before. In Tabriz, people had looked festive, their arms full of presents to take to relatives. Now they looked serious, almost angry. Near the platform huge black flags with colored calligraphy were stacked and next to them bouquets of chains, anchored in wooden handles.

"Follow me," said Ameer.

Matt followed blindly.

"Where are we going?" he finally asked.

"My uncle has a stall in the bazaar."

Without explanation Ameer quickened his pace. Others were running too. The stalls around them all looked closed and Matt wondered why they were coming here. Shop after shop had the shutters pulled down. But Ameer pressed on.

Matt began to sweat. He would never be able to find his way out again. Not alone, anyway. These old bazaars were labyrinths built in the oldest parts of town, often adjacent to mosques. Only belatedly did Matt realize that the marches would probably start right here.

Finally they came to a shop where the shutter was not completely pulled down.

Ameer said something in Turkish into the dark and two men came out. Matt stared at them. They were swarthy-looking, with days' worth of stubble on their cheeks. They wore hats pulled down over their foreheads and there was a Mafioso look about them that made Matt nervous. They grabbed his luggage and handed it in under the shutter to the inside of the shop.

"Ameerl Welcome! How are you? Are you well? *Salaam aleikum*," they cried, embracing him.

"My teacher, Mr. Matthew, has come with me."

Matt nodded politely, but the two men grabbed his hand in turn and shook it warmly. Ameer began talking to his uncles in Azeri Turkish. It was a language Matt barely knew, although it was the language of the villagers. The Peace Corps had trained him mostly in Persian.

Matt sipped carefully from the tiny gold-rimmed tea glass they handed him, choosing a big lump of *qand* to hold between his teeth while the hot acrid liquid melted the sugar. He was waiting. Soon they would start offering him some goods. Rugs, probably. Or maybe jewelry. Hard to tell what they were selling here. But it wouldn't matter really. A foreigner, even an unemployed foreigner, ought to be good for some kind of sale.

Matt's vision hadn't quite adjusted from the light outside. All he could see in the dimness were a bunch of burlap sacks. These didn't reassure him. He recalled the time he had crossed the border into Pakistan and seen a couple of thuggish looking types carrying burlap sacks like these.

Then a scent came to him, making him realize they were near to the spice sellers. He sniffed again and realized it was turmeric, a spice he'd never really smelled before he came to Iran. Now its cool mustiness would forever remind him of the bazaar.

The three men were talking among themselves. Abruptly they stopped and turned toward Matt.

They were looking at his clothes, his glasses. "I don't know," one of them was saying. "Are you sure?" Ameer was gazing at him and smiling.

Matt's heart lurched. He put the glass down. "*Baw ayjahzay*," he said, using the polite formula for leave-taking as he stood up.

He was already ducking under the partly closed shutter when he felt the ground shake. In the next second came the thunderous voices and footfalls of the marchers.

"Ya Hossein! Ya Hossein!"

Matt pulled himself hastily back into the shop.

Ameer came over to him. "Why are you trying to leave?" he asked in English. "You are my uncles' guest."

Before Matt could answer one of the uncles put his hands on Matt's shirt, a wool shirt, one of his good ones. A Pendleton plaid such as no Iranian would ever wear.

"You must remove it," one of the men was telling him, and before Matt could say anything, they carefully pulled off his shirt. Underneath he wore a faded McGovern campaign tee.

One of the men shook his head. Off went the tee-shirt. Matt was shivering, from fear as much as cold.

But before he could make a move, the uncle had snatched off his glasses. "Don't worry," he said in Persian.

After that they pushed him out into the corridor where they stood on either side of him. Someone shoved a wooden handle into his hand. Attached was a bunch of small metal chains.

"Ya Hossein!" roared a new throng coming up behind them.

When they reached the rug shop, the four of them fell into step. Matt was afraid to look from side to side so at first all he did was march. But then, gradually, he understood what the chains were for.

His throat opened and he felt his own voice joining the chant "Ya Hossein, Ya Hossein." This was punctuated by the rhythm of chains raised first to slap one shoulder and then the other.

When he had been pushed into the march all he had felt was terror. But now, inexplicably, the fear drained away. For the first time since he had come to this country he felt himself utterly a part of it, the way he had felt at campus demonstrations a few years earlier. Joining the anti-Vietnam War marches had been a cathartic thing for him. A feeling that he was part of something larger. A feeling that he was at one with others who shared his beliefs.

But of course it was more than that. He had seen first hand how people were oppressed here. It didn't matter how many centuries had passed, they were still under the yoke of the dictators who had killed their beloved caliph.

The rhythm of this march entered his body as he chanted with the others. His voice seemed to leave his throat of its own accord. So also did his arms rise as he began slapping first one shoulder and then the other.

Matt wasn't sure when he started to smell blood. At first he saw it only on the others, blurrily, in streaks, running down men's faces, criss-crossing their chests. They were coming out of the bazaar where the sun made the white garb of the men seem even brighter with the blotches of red blooming against the fabric.

Matt felt something run into his eyes and put his finger up to catch it. Sweat, he had thought at first. But when he peered at his finger he saw it was stained in red.

By the time they came back to the shop, Matt wondered if the dizziness he felt could be from the loss of blood. But the wound turned out to be superficial although Ameer made a big fuss about it, dabbing it repeatedly with alcohol until it burned.

Matt hooked his glasses back over his ears and stared at the men next to him. Their faces appeared disconcertingly close. He could smell their sweat too.

"Are you OK?" Ameer asked, his face creased with worry. "Maybe we should take you to a doctor, yes?"

Matt shook his head.

Finally one of the uncles spoke.

Ameer translated. "My uncle wants to know if you are *Musulman*?"

The adrenaline was still pumping, but Matt could feel the fatigue underneath. He shook his head.

Ameer gave a nervous smile. "I tell them before, but they not believe. You understand our suffering."

Later, when Matt had his plaid shirt back on and they were out walking on the street to the uncle's house, passersby stared at his head bandage. Ameer held his hand, the way men did here. Matt felt utterly exhausted. But there was still a feast to get through. Everyone stood when he came through the doorway into the humble room where, judging from all the footwear neatly lined up on the mat, many bodies lived crowded together.

The food revived him and he lay back on the floor gathering his strength for the evening flight.

All around him the conversation of the men buzzed, most of it in Azeri Turkish. But then the room fell silent and the oldest man there spoke. Ameer answered and then turned to Matt.

"He asks why you care so much about Hossein and the people of Iran?'

Matt looked around at the circle of rugged faces with jutting cheekbones and bodies that had no extra flesh on them. He stared at the saffron-dyed rice still mounded on the serving platters and the sucked bones tossed on individual plates. He thought of the two story colonial house with pillars where he had grown up and the meals seated around the oversized polished mahogany table.

Finally he answered. "Because it isn't right."

There was murmuring all around the room after Ameer translated and he wondered how they interpreted his answer. He had used the present tense, but the murder of Hossein had happened centuries ago.

Still later, on the way to Mehrabad Airport, Matt asked his student why.

"Why what?" Ameer asked, drawing his heavy black eyebrows

together.

"Why did you invite me to come your uncles' shop? Did you know I would be part of the marches?"

Ameer was silent for so long, Matt thought he wasn't going to answer.

Finally he said, "You are a good man, Mr. Mattoo."

Matt waited, not liking what this presaged. He was a stupid man was what he was thinking to himself. One who blundered about and took unnecessary chances.

Then finally Ameer began to speak. "I worry about you."

"Why?" Matt asked, but he already knew.

Ameer didn't elaborate. He went on. "In my country, we call on Hossein to help us in our hour of need."

Matt looked at him. They were in the back of a taxi and the driver was watching them in the mirror. Matt had no idea whether or not he understood English.

Ameer said, "We organize too, here, in my country. Like your Talking Union."

Matt nodded, suddenly understanding that these marches were not about what had happened seven centuries ago.

"We show that we are ready to die, if it is necessary." Ameer said this almost in an undertone.

Matt felt the hairs rise on the back of his neck and then shame engulfed him. So many dangers awaited Ameer. Dangers that, again, Matt should have thought about when he was in the village.

Getting thrown out of the country was nothing. He understood that now.

They walked into the terminal where Ameer insisted on carrying his bag. Matt couldn't wrest it away from him. As they waited he thought about what he could say or offer in recompense for the gift he'd been given.

Finally his flight was called.

"Goodbye Mr. Mattoo," Ameer said, taking his hand and then leaning forward and kissing him on first one cheek and than another.

Tears came to Matt's eyes and he tried to blink them away. But Ameer saw them and a smile came to his lips.

Later when Matt thought about it he realized that none of it had been about words. Words were cheap. It was blood and tears and the willingness to lay down your life that mattered in the long run. The men who had made the unions happen had realized this too. The song had made it sound so simple – too simple, Matt realized now. As if you could articulate what was right and what was wrong and then lay it on people like a prescription.

Ameer had laid Moharrem on him. Matt touched the wound on his forehead and a part of him hoped there would be a scar, like a bizarre souvenir he could brag about. Like the old adventurer Sir Richard Burton who had managed to pull off pretending to be Muslim in order to get into Mecca and Medina.

But the world wasn't that simple anymore. People had come too close to one another, and yet they seemed further away from one another than ever. Matt laid his head against the glass of the airplane window and felt an incredible sadness well up. He wasn't finished with this land and these people, but they were finished with him. Tears welled up again and he let them fall this time as he stared down through the cloudless sky at the bare earth below.

# *How to Come Back to Earth*

## *by Jessica Bozek*

On the 30th anniversary of the Challenger explosion, NPR interviews one of the scientists who failed to persuade NASA officials that launching the space shuttle would be a disaster. My daughter wants to know where the astronauts died—in the sky or in the ocean. She asks to see body parts, believing pictures of everything she imagines exist on my computer. Probably they do.

We look at Christa McAuliffe in a blue jumpsuit. Her permed hair reminds me of the crying teachers who huddled together in the hallway of my elementary school. And of my mother, who watched the terrible footage with me when I got home.

The next morning my daughter vows to be a "rocketship scientist." She will tell the astronauts that the spaceship shouldn't go up in the sky. They'll listen to the rules and they won't have to die.

*

There is too much silk, so I sew my mother a parachute. I think thick seams might hold more air, keep her aloft.

We pull out her IV and strap the parachute to her back, then climb steep red stairs to the attic. I open a window. She sighs. Wind catches her breath and the canopy fills.

Dense clouds weight the sky. The canopy crumples from its apex. Tumors drop from my mother's torso, as if she is being slowly wrung out. Updrafts snap against silk, until the parachute is an orange husk on snow.

# *Parnassus*

## *by Michelle McGurk*

The year my father moved to Oregon, I asked Santa to bring me a puppy. When he didn't deliver, I began my lobbying campaign.

I had the perfect dog in mind—a Scottish terrier I'd call Blackie—and I drew pictures of me and Jenny Yamaguchi walking him around our old neighborhood together with Lucky, the fluffy white Westie she got for Christmas. I stressed to everyone involved that I preferred a Scottie, but I wasn't picky. I'd take whatever mutt needed rescuing from the pound.

"Our apartment is too small," Mom said.

My older brother added, "I'm not cleaning up dog crap."

Grandma hung my drawings on her refrigerator, the only note of disorder in her otherwise immaculate kitchen, but Grandpa followed up with a resounding *no* when I suggested keeping a dog at their house. "You're only here on holidays," he said. "Who's going to take care of a puppy the rest of the year?"

Then there was Dad, on the phone from Ashland, Oregon. He'd gotten a big break. He'd be playing Tom Snout in *A Midsummer*

*Night's Dream*, which meant we'd have to postpone my summer visitation until at least Christmas.

"And then we can get a dog?" I said.

"I had a dog once, Rosie. A Golden Retriever named Parnassus," he said. "Oh, the adventures we had! Me and that dog…we set out one day to climb to the top of Resurrection Hill, and, sure enough, we got lost. The sun set, and I knew my folks would be sore worried. But wouldn't you know, the moon shone full that night, and the stars as bright as icicles. We had to ford a stream—twice!—but old Parnassus found our way home. My mother, God rest her soul, was half crazy with worry. She saw my wet shoes and clothes and started hollering. She raised her arm to whip my sorry butt, but Parnassus stepped between us and nosed Mother's hand out of the way.

"Lovebug, that dog truly was man's best friend."

That was the great thing about my dad. He knew what it was to want something with your whole heart. He knew how to turn wishes into reality.

"Poor Parnassus." Dad cleared his throat twice. "There was a fight with a raccoon, and she ended up getting rabies. In the end, there was nothing the vet could do."

I could hear him sniffling.

"A child never gets over losing their dog," Dad said. "I don't want to see you go through that, sweetheart. I couldn't bear to watch your heart break."

My ninth birthday arrived on September 5. My grandparents gave me a tartan skirt and red sweater with a black dog knitted onto the chest, and Grandma baked an angel-food cake. After dessert, Mom was in Grandpa's office for a long while.

"Rosie, come talk to Daddy." Mom's voice was bright and loud. "He called to wish you a happy birthday."

I hadn't heard the phone ring. The receiver was warm from my mother's ear.

"I didn't get a puppy," I told my father. "And Mom says I can't buy one with the money you sent."

"The money?"

"Thanks, Daddy. The card was really nice, too."

"Read it to me."

"You picked it out."

"I had so much trouble deciding this time," Dad said. "I was standing there in the store, and it was five minutes before closing time, and nothing seemed just right. So I closed my eyes and spun around and pointed to one card. Sometimes, Rosie, you have to leave things to fate."

"Can you do your lines again?"

"Show's over, kiddo."

"Please, Dad. *In this same interlude it doth befall that I, one Snout by name—"*

"We shouldn't run up your Grandma's phone bill."

"Okay. I'll send you a letter soon. I love you."

In October, I brought Mr. Bigwig home from school with me. He was a fat brown rabbit with white feet and a white patch over one eye. I told my mother that he was on loan from Mrs. Cortez, my fourth grade teacher, that each of the kids got to take him home for two weeks. The truth was, Ross Claypool had developed an allergy and his parents' attorney sent a letter to the principal threatening to sue the Berkeley Unified School District if Mr. Bigwig and his friend Fiver didn't disappear.

Half the class volunteered to provide new homes, and Mrs. Cortez drew names from a jar. I really wanted the tiny Fiver, who raced around the classroom when let out of his cage, begging for treats from our lunchboxes, but he went to Linh Vo, who lived in the building across the street from ours.

"That's not fair," Mike A. said. "She's just going to eat it for dinner."

"Tastes just like dog," Mike S. said.

"Boys, enough!" Mrs. Cortez wrote *Mike S* on the chalkboard. Mike A's name was already there. Mrs. Cortez gave him another check mark, which meant detention. Linh and I smiled at each other across the room. Every day that the Mikes had detention was a day we could walk home in peace.

The next day, Linh arranged for her aunt to drive us home. Mrs. Cortez gave us the rabbits' wire cages and water bottles and divided the bag of pellets and the wood shavings for the bottom of the cages.

Linh helped me carry Mr. Bigwig and his things upstairs. I had never invited her inside before. I wasn't supposed to have anyone over while my mother was at school.

"Your apartment is huge," she said. "I can't believe only three people live here."

Alan and I had our own small rooms, but our mother slept in the living room on a foldout couch. "You should have seen my old house," I said. "It had two bathrooms and a backyard big enough for two dogs."

Mr. Bigwig sat on my lap each afternoon while I read, burrowing into my comforter and eating carrots out of my hand. He was a docile roommate, except in the early mornings and evenings, when he'd jump up onto my bed and run laps around my bedroom (or the living room when my mother wasn't home). He had a way of switching directions mid-air, twisting his body and wriggling his butt, jumping for sheer joy. Sometimes I detected a hint of attitude—*I've got a tail and you don't*—and sometimes he paused and nudged my leg or foot as if he wanted me to leap with him.

Sometimes he flopped next to me, out of breath and heart beating as fast as hummingbird wings. Sometimes—and I would think of this move years later when I took yoga classes—Mr. Bigwig would stretch his whole spine, planting his front paws in the carpet and uncoiling each vertebrae like a wave.

Linh and I compared notes. Fiver did the same thing, always at the same time of day. It made her uncles crazy.

Mrs. Cortez told us that rabbits are crepuscular, and she offered extra credit if we would write a report.

*Crepuscular animals play and eat during twilight hours. Twilight includes the early morning, before dawn.* (I'd always thought it was evening, when I turned on all the lights in the apartment and checked the lock on the door, counted the minutes until my mother or Alan came home.) *The crepuscular trait evolved to prevent rabbits from becoming prey to larger animals like coyotes and hawks.*

Like me, Linh liked dictionary words. She liked reading, too, and I loaned her my Narnia books and *Anne of Green Gables*, which came back with nibble marks on the corners.

"I'm sorry," she said. "Fiver did it. I'll get you a new one."

"It doesn't matter," I said. "Biggie ate half the cover of *Ballet Shoes*. Have you read that yet?"

In addition to books, Mr. Bigwig chewed through the shoelaces on Alan's sneakers and gnawed on the leg of the coffee table. Once, I found him behind my bedroom door, tearing out strands of shag carpet with his teeth and front paws. It was all a small price for the nose nudging my face in the morning, urging me to wake up, for the feel of warm soft fur under my fingertips while I read or watched television.

On Thursdays, my mother had class until 9 p.m., and I spent the afternoons alone reading until my eyes crossed and my stomach rumbled, at which point I would heat up a TV dinner. Alan was usually off on his bike with his crowd of skinny boys.

I walked home from school with Linh, and she told me she'd taught Fiver to sit on his hind legs and beg for a vegetable scrap. "He eats rice out of my hand. Now when my grandma cooks, he comes running and begs," she said. "It's so cute."

"Do you want to come over?" I asked her.

"I have to go to catechism," she said. "Maybe another day. I can bring Fiver, too."

I climbed the two flights of stairs, waved to Mrs. Holmes who was watching television with her front door open. I unlocked the door. The guy next door was playing the Eagles—Tequila Sunrise—so loud that I could hear them singing after I closed the door.

I left my library books on the coffee table and got a carrot out of the refrigerator. At my bedroom door, I paused with my hand on the knob and positioned my body in the doorjamb, ready to block Mr. Bigwig with my foot if he tried to escape.

I heard no scurrying, just the hollow swoosh of the door scraping the shag carpet. I didn't see Mr. Bigwig until I closed the door. He was lying on his side in the corner where he had harvested the carpet strands.

I dropped the carrot and knelt beside him. "Mr. Bigwig? Hey, Biggie." I spoke in the cooing voice I used when we played. "Biggie-boy, are you awake?"

I stretched my hand toward him, jerked it away, then forced my index finger to the tip of the fur on his side. Even at his sleepiest, any touch, even the hovering hint of a touch, launched Mr. Bigwig into activity (or sent him to running to hide under my bed).

I stared at his white chest and belly. A rabbit's heart can beat 130 to 325 times in a single minute. In that same sixty seconds, it breathes 30 to 60 times. Mrs. Cortez had us fill out a chart comparing the respiration rates of different species. She taught us to place our index and middle fingers across the inside of our wrists or over the carotid artery beneath our jaws and count our own heartbeats while the second hand of the wall clock swept forward ten seconds. Sometimes when Mr. Bigwig flopped next to me after racing back and forth, showing how he could jump over my legs, I would rest my hand on his back, feeling his rapid flutter racing against the slower pulse in my wrist.

Now I didn't check Mr. Bigwig's pulse. I didn't need to.

I wondered how long he had been lying alone. I whispered, "I'm sorry."

I looked at the clock. 3:50. Five hours before Mom was home. I had time to take care of this before she found out.

I picked up my old blankie from the end of my bed and held it to my face. It was threadbare in places, the satin edging worn through and frayed, and Mr. Bigwig had nibbled a hole in one corner. Grandma kept threatening to throw it away. I smelled the years on the blanket, then draped it over Mr. Bigwig's body before I could change my mind. I got a shopping bag with handles from underneath the kitchen sink, used the edge of a cookie sheet to slide Mr. Bigwig into the bag.

Two blocks from our apartment was a vacant lot, several acres in size, waiting to be developed. Old-timers like Mrs. Holmes said there had once been a Victorian mansion on the property, and in places, traces of the brick foundation remained. At the back of the lot, was a cluster of eucalyptus trees, the entrance to a culvert, and a small creek. It was the same creek that ran through the neighborhood, bisecting backyards and twisting through tunnels underneath parking lots and sidewalks. Sometimes after a rainstorm, Linh and I could hear its water rushing underground as we walked home from school or the library.

I'd been down to the empty lot with my brother and his friends, but never alone. It was a deserted place, and we'd seen squirrels and raccoons there, and once, a small wild rabbit. It would be the perfect spot to bury Mr. Bigwig.

We didn't have a shovel, so I took the metal spoon Mom used to stir soup and Alan's Swiss Army knife. I tucked my copy of *The Velveteen Rabbit* in the bag next to Mr. Bigwig's body. I had this idea that I would cover him with dirt and leaves and read the ending where the stuffed rabbit becomes real, before saying goodbye. I knew *Watership Down* would have been more fitting, but I didn't own a copy, and there wasn't time to make it to the library before dark.

At the eucalyptus trees, I walked in a slow circle, testing the ground with the toe of my sneaker. I found a soft muddy spot, looped the bag over my shoulder, and knelt to poke at the dirt.

I heard splashing in the shallow creek, a sharp bark, then a flash of brown and white and black at my feet. A dog sniffed and jumped up on me, putting muddy paws on my thighs.

"Down, boy. Go home." I shoved at him with both hands.

One of the twine handles broke on the shopping bag, and the dog lunged at it.

"Scram! Go away!" I twisted away from him, holding the bag—and Mr. Bigwig—close to my chest.

A second dog appeared, growling, and jumped at my back. Both of their snouts and front paws knocked at the bag and my torso. I saw teeth, wet eyes, and I froze.

The bag hit the ground. The metal spoon and the book slid out. I could see Mr. Bigwig's hind foot from beneath my yellow blanket. The dogs saw him too, or smelled him. They lunged forward, shoving me aside and ripping into the package.

My tennis shoes stuck in the soft ground like it was concrete. I saw blood and fur, heard voices, the rough tones of men or teenage boys, yelling and calling names.

"Duke, Lucky, get back here."

The smaller dog looked at me and let out a low grrr, then bounded toward the voices. I felt my feet unglue and I ran, behind the trees and around the perimeter of the lot, trying to stay out of sight.

It was uphill to our apartment, and I ran the whole way, empty-handed. The denim of my jeans chafed my thighs. I touched the inside of my pant leg and discovered that somewhere in the tumble of paws and teeth, my bladder had let go.

I washed up at the bathroom sink and put Neosporin on the scrapes on my arms. Dirty clothes went into a garbage bag, along with the washcloth and everything Mr. Bigwig had touched. Water bottle, food bowl, the toilet paper rolls he liked to play with, an empty Kleenex box—I dragged it all down to the dumpster behind our building, came back with his cage and left it next to a broken television set.

Upstairs, I wrapped myself in my old sleeping bag and watched television until my brother came home. I forgot to eat dinner, and Alan didn't ask. He went in his room and played guitar for half an hour with the door closed.

When he emerged, he glanced at my open door. "Shouldn't you be in bed?"

"I'm not tired."

"You don't have the bun out here, do you? Mom will be pissed if there's rabbit shit in the couch again."

"He's gone." My voice caught, and I swallowed hard. "My turn was up. I had to take him back to school."

"I was just getting used to the little turd." He fake-punched my arm, then knocked my feet off the couch. "Make some room, dipshit."

He pretended to grab my sleeping bag. I tugged back, then shoved his thighs with my feet.

"Don't hog it, assface," I said.

"It's all yours." Alan squeezed my bare foot. We stayed up watching *Hill Street Blues* until the news came on and we heard Mom's footsteps on the breezeway.

"Run and get in bed," Alan said. "I'm not getting busted for letting you stay up."

Over Christmas break, Alan had a basketball tournament he couldn't miss, so I flew to Oregon alone. Dad met my plane in Portland, and there was a young woman with him—Alison—who had feathered hair and a swath of beetle-green shadow on each eyelid. She pulled me into a quick hug and I could feel the round swell of her belly beneath her corduroy jumper.

It was over an hour to Dad's new house. On the way there, he drove past a two-story beige building. "That's the place, kiddo," he said. "Can you believe it? Go in to renew your car insurance, meet the love of your life, and find a new career."

They were getting married on New Year's Eve. I was to be the flower girl.

"Does Mom know?" I asked.

"I asked her not to tell you. We wanted to wait 'til you were here."

Dad's right hand was on the gearshift, and Alison placed hers on top of it. "We wanted to tell you in person," she said.

Their new house was as square and beige as the office building, with a flat roof and a carport, but no garage.

"Three bedrooms," Dad said. "Plans are to add another bathroom soon."

At the front door, he gave the keys to Alison and covered my eyes with his hands. "Santa came early," he said.

I heard a tinny bark, toenails skittering on wood, Dad saying, "Down, boy!" and then "Surprise!" as paws and a wet nose bounced against my shins.

"Falstaff, down! Be good now!" Alison said.

"He's a Jack Russell, smart as a whip," Dad said.

The dog whirled and yipped around me, jumped up and begged for attention, his nails scratching my bare legs. I stood like a statue, felt my father watching me, felt my eyes go hot and body turn cold.

"He's cute," I said pushing the words past the tears in my throat.

Dad grinned and Alison grabbed my wrist and pulled me closer to the yapping dog. "He wants to play with you, Rosie. Let him sniff your hand. He needs to get used to you."

She talked baby talk to the dog while she held the stiff rod of my arm in a strong grip, her fingers around my wrist forcing my hand to splay wide. I could feel each hot and sandpapery lick.

"Nice doggy. There's a sweet doggy." I worked to fill my voice with delight. "Thank you, Daddy. He's what I've always wanted."

After my father married Alison, cards arrived a week before my birthday and holidays too, postmarked and with a ten-dollar bill inside. The first one came on Valentine's Day, and I taped it on my wall next to the picture of me and Dad that Alison had taken before their courthouse wedding.

That summer, I had a new baby brother (and another the next summer), but Falstaff was gone. Mrs. Cortez had given us a list of books—Recommended Reading for Fifth Grade—before we left for summer vacation, and I was allowed to walk to the library by myself, to read quietly while the baby was napping. I read every book on the list, even *Old Yeller*, although I was thinking about Mr. Bigwig when I got to the sad parts.

I left the book lying about the house, on the coffee table and in the dining room. I sat on the couch and pretended to read it while

Dad watched a baseball game.

"Did Falstaff get rabies, too?" I finally asked.

"What gave you that idea?" Dad said. "I told you, Rosie, we took him out to the country, to live on a farm."

"Is it like Grandpa's farm?" I asked.

"Bigger," Dad said. "There are acres and acres where he can run and play. Cows and sheep, and oak trees too. A pond he can swim in. Jackrabbits he can chase."

I didn't ask if we could visit.

As for Linh Vo, she was the only one I told about Mr. Bigwig—but only that he had passed, not the details of the attempted burial or his final disposal. I went to her apartment after school, and we fed Fiver slices of apple and carrot; she came to mine, and I showed her the picture of Dad and Alison. She told me her father was in Thailand waiting to move to America.

She showed me the tadpoles her cousins had caught in the creek. They swam in an old mayonnaise jar, turning into frogs, one leg at a time. "We should catch some before they're gone," Linh said.

"I don't want to run into the Mikes. They hang out there all the time."

We walked to the library instead and checked out Beverly Cleary books.

In the summer, while I was visiting Dad or my grandparents, Linh moved away. That was the way of our neighborhood. Families moved in and out, even in the middle of the school year, sometimes in the middle of the night.

Years later, I spotted Linh and my old friend Jenny Yamaguchi at the freshman orientation for Presentation High School. They lived two blocks from each other, Linh's aunt and uncle having bought a house in the neighborhood where I'd lived before my parents' divorce.

Linh didn't have Fiver anymore. Her aunt hadn't wanted pets in the new house.

"I wanted to leave him with you, but you weren't home," Linh told me. "So I took him down to the vacant lot and set him free."

"We saw him once." I'd never gone back to the vacant lot, but I continued my story. "He was hopping across the grass, then he ran under some bushes. I told my brother: 'That rabbit looks just like Linh's little Fiver.' There were other bunnies with him, maybe two or three. They seemed so happy."

# *poem) (from next summer : kilowatt-green variant*

*by Marco Maisto*

untraceable muscle
wave-beaten tracer-boy
muscle sound gameday
kilowatt yellow
untoneable man
kilowatt red
who are you not
untraceable man
but synch me and shower
endgame-white fix me
overrun hex knot

finch colored core
kilowatt female
muscular trace
wrist burn romantic
overtuned gameboy
yeah yr going too
gameboy-gray fissure
oh you're going too?
suggestible echodome
as if just to suppose
finch me once more

killowatt click-dress
ice-cube blue you
uninterrupt
exorbital teal
uninterrupt
seashell teal hair
familiar blue werewolf
eyelightning first date
motel red sunset
new zipcode turquoise
purple-grey sometimes

eyelightning crimson
endgame-white promise
white matter prelude
black matter prelude
dark matter indigo
humming green birdnote
off-the-shelf footprint
now synch me and shatter
hot home-made viewpoint
exorbital teal
untraceable girl

# *poem) (from next season:*

## *by Dina Hardy*

**A palimpsest of the previous poem**

| | |
|---|---|
| poem) | (from next season : |
| kilowatt-green | outerbanks variant) |
| | |
| trace | kite string to key quays |
| wave-beaten | hurricane's coming |
| sound | swells in tattered silk |
| low | provenance unknown |
| to | ruin-mute scrutiny |
| kilowatt | horizon locked gate |
| | knock sea did you lock the gate? |
| un | knock pulse memory |
| synch | now and next against |
| white | ocean-pulse in echo |
| overrun | clocks twisted string |
| | |
| finch | wings in wind fury squall |
| kilowatt | desire crash rocks |
| trace | my skin tide-pool pull |
| wrist burn romantic | fingers circle |
| over | heartbeat unbound |
| going | rush and release |
| fissure | forceful delirious rain |
| you're | holding tight to comet tail veil |
| echodome | sculpting stone's past |
| to suppose | our imagined future |

| | |
|---|---|
| once more | in warning's embrace |
| | |
| click | tic-talk under deep rumor |
| you | a stone's weight ripple blue |
| interrupt | offshore rainband swirl |
| orbit | scyclone-eye keyhole |
| inter | —rupt —view —twine |
| hair | to string storm's flight |
| familiar | locks release in underwater waves |
| eyelightning | waterworks reshape |
| motel red sunset | that was then now |
| new | syntax space station |
| purple-grey sometimes | seaweed lullaby in reverse |
| | |
| light | sometimes unfolds |
| endgame- promise | in reverse origami sky |
| prelude | flightless animals rainfall |
| prelude | then thunderclap |
| dark matter | dangerous weather |
| green note | gunpowder explosion |
| the | want to drown in heat |
| now synch me and shatter | me in derivation fracture |
| me | in two with kilowatt- |
| teal | chromakey electricity with an |
| untraceable | kite's flight in fever kiss |

# *Someone Called for You*

## *by Shane Delaney*

1

When she turned the corner in the store, holding two gallons of paint in one hand and a box of rainbow chalk in the other, I realized I'd dreamt about her the night before. In my dream, I was still married to her, and we were in a cornfield that was suspended hundreds of feet in the sky. It was warm. We were sweaty and smiling as we harvested cherry tomatoes from cornstalks. Terri, I said, and woke up.

Here in front of me, she looked bright and fit and tan, the pale office skin and dry hair gone, a thin flannel shirt and her blonde hair loosely up, a smear of dirt along her jaw. Terri, I said, and she smiled, though her eyes flicked down to the badge, to the fat leather belt of my uniform. I was the same, she was new.

We're trying a farm stand, she said, holding up the paint, a thin, hard muscle in her arm as she did.

That's good, I said. I was flushed, my head light from being close to her again.

You're like a different person. I barely got it out before my throat tightened. I wanted to compliment her on getting the farm going, committing to a real life change. But I just stood there in my stiff blue uniform, pressed and thick and wearing me. It had never felt so conspicuous, so clownish.

*I'm proud of you. Take me with you. I love you, you're gorgeous, you left me.*

She stood calmly, even and square, offering the patience for me left from our old love, and my dream came back, and we were in the sky again, the warm air, picking tomatoes in the clouds.

The gravelly scratch of my radio cut in:

Millsy, you near Garden St? Head that way, we need your translation. Over.

And my little trance fell away. We were in the bright, narrow hall of the hardware store, stacked boxes of screws and washers, tarps and drop cloths, marking paint and dryer vents. I touched her elbow as a goodbye, turned, and pinched the mic on my shoulder, ducking down the next aisle before speaking into it.

2

I drove around back of the body shop and parked the cruiser alongside a knotted collection of shitboxes in various states of repair and Barry Tuck's bright orange Ford Super Duty. On the truck's door, painted in blocky black lettering: Tuck Landscaping. I passed the wide, dented garage doors of the shop and headed for the office, which you had to go through to get to Barry's apartment. It was Saturday in the evening, and the place was empty.

The stairs leading up were narrow, old plywood treads painted a dark brown, chipping and dusty. My mind was replaying Cheryl's blubbering 911 call that they patched to me because, for some reason, the town had always considered Barry and I friends.

Cheryl, sweetheart, it's Mills.

I could picture the running mascara and bleached hair. She wailed my name snottily, saying it more like Bills than Mills.

Easy Cheryl, eeeeasy sweetheart, it's gonna be fine. Breathe, honey.

But she just kept saying heesga over and over.

I told her to try to say it another way.

Warry, she said. *Barry*.

I drew my gun and pointed it at the floor, but then re-holstered it. Barry was 5'6" and keg-shaped; he'd never posed an actual physical threat to anyone, despite his loud voice and shit-talking. Still, my breathing had taken on a quick little rhythm. I inhaled deeply to interrupt it.

Barry, I called from the top step. I knocked on the door, forced myself to call louder and knocked twice more. No answer. I'm coming in, Barry, put your pants on. I opened the door.

The inside of Barry's place looked more like a storage unit than an apartment. He was never a man to take rejection well, and when Cheryl had sent him packing, he'd crammed everything he could into Jimmy Young's attic. This had created a pretty significant logistical challenge: moving from a two-bedroom ranch to a 475 square foot pitched-ceiling loft. The result was an apartment that looked like the basement of the Museum of Bad Taste: green suede love seats stacked up, tin signs advertising beer and motor oil leaned against walls, a velvet painting of a stalking leopard, a six foot tall cherry-red gumball machine, and colorful dots of crap amongst the rows and stacks of cardboard boxes that filled almost every square inch aside from the bed, which lay empty and unmade. He'd been living there temporarily for two years.

I was able to determine that Cheryl had called Barry eight times between last night and this evening with no answer.

Then she had added something else and I asked her to repeat it, but only because I needed a second to process what she'd said.

Andy had been right to patch the call in to me; I was good at translating that sloppy language.

I'd spent a decent amount of time with Barry and Cheryl when they were still married, but all of it had been on duty, breaking up fights between the two of them. I'd head over after one of them finally stopped bluffing about calling the cops and break up their latest shit storm that wasn't actually about what either of them thought it was about. Once, Barry was armed with a rolling pin, Cheryl wielding a barstool like a lion tamer, and they'd screamed at me that they were fighting about the toaster setting.

And here I was again, listening to her blob words at me.

I fink—heshaw—himsa, she said a little more slowly, a wet sob sucked up in the middle. I'd heard it right the first time.

*I think he shot himself.*

3

I called his name again, and again got no answer. I moved further into the apartment. The boxes, stacked six feet high, created nothing but blind spots and shadows. I was waiting for an arm slung out on the floor or the thick edge of pooled blood.

On the back side of the room by the windows was a flimsy folding table that had a hot plate, a breadbox, and a microwave, the door of which was swung open to reveal the red splatter of over-nuked pizza on the inside. Next to the table was the slop sink I had helped Jimmy install when he'd converted the space. The sink was cruddy now, no longer new, full of caked dishes and Styrofoam takeout containers.

The only other room was the bathroom. *The suicide room*, some guys called it. I'd left the bathroom for last, but I should have gone there first and gotten it over with. The door was closed. I put my ear up to it. There was a humming, like an exhaust fan, only higher pitched.

I knew I should go in, but there was something about Barry being dead on the other side of that door that bothered me too much to go ahead. I had felt so badly for him for so many years, for as long as I'd known him. He'd never had the life he wanted, and now he'd ended it.

I'd always hated that people considered Barry and me friends.

I leaned my shoulder against the door, took hold of the knob, which was warm and slightly damp. I gutted myself up with a final, deep inhale-exhale and swung the door open:

There was fog on the mirror and condensation on the faucet, a bottle of Powers whiskey on the toilet tank, smoke in the air, water on the floor at the foot of the tub. Silence, aside from the squealy humming. A leg hung over the edge of the tub—

And Barry Tuck, smoking a cigar, wearing neon-green plastic headphones and scrubbing his armpit with a loofah.

Jesus Christ! he yelled, ripping the headphones off, the squealy humming turning into some '80s hair band rock guitar solo.

I slumped against the sink. Barry sat up in the soapy tub, waiting for an explanation with his arms stretched out and his palms up. I grabbed the whiskey and tried to pour a capful, but my hands were too shaky so I set it back down.

You finally making a move on me, Millsy? he asked with a smirk. Hop in here, you sexy bastard!

You don't answer your phone anymore?

In the tub?

Half the town probably thinks you're dead by this point.

Barry smiled with a sort of inquisitive pride. When I told him we had received a suicide call, the smile dropped.

That psycho witch, he said.

Well, Barry, hold on. She called out of concern. You should've heard her crying. She was terrified.

Oh, she cries like that when she burns toast.

Well you're right up there with toast, then, I said, but Barry didn't laugh. Come on, I said.

Fuck you, Mills, you know how goddamn embarrassing this is? I'm a businessman in this town. I have a sterling-silver reputation.

He tossed his cigar into the water. It hissed and the end went gray. He added, Well, I *had* a sterling-silver reputation.

You're not a heart surgeon, Barry. Get your pudgy ass outta there. Time to make a phone call.

Holy shit, he said. Nice relaxing Saturday.

I pinched the little mic on my shoulder to call it in.

Andy, we're good here. Barry is alive and well and clean as a whistle. Call Cheryl and let her know.

4

A few minutes later we were in Barry's sort-of kitchen. Barry wore a navy blue robe and gray sweatpants, his beer gut pushing out of the opening. He stood in front of the breadbox and looked out the window at the wrecked cars and oil puddles in the unpaved lot. I leaned against the slop sink.

You need to give Cheryl a ring.

Fat fucking chance.

I looked around again at the boxes and thought about my house: I kept it neat, but compared to Barry's place, my living room looked like they'd just filmed an ad for a vacuum cleaner. It made me thankful—it was good to know it was waiting for me across town. I tried to imagine what was in the boxes, all the things Barry and Cheryl had acquired—Barry's remote control cars, the bocce set they had in the side yard, tank tops that said CAPE COD, a half-finished wedding album that had been the central prop in one fight I'd broken up. All of it jammed in there, pieces pushed up against one another in the darkness.

Barry started speculating about the chatter that must be buzzing around town right now: apparently Barry Tuck jumped off the body shop roof and broke his neck. You hear Barry shot himself in the head? He really seemed to be taking to the idea of being dead, or at least being thought of as dead. He had received the Big Call from God Himself and now had a celebrity friend that no one in town could top, not even George Grier, whose wife's second cousin had married Larry Bird.

The whole town's going to be talking about this, huh, Barry said.

As long as it can beat out the current Big News.

What?

Mrs. Jergins drove her Plymouth Caravelle through the front window of Supreme Donuts.

He asked me what Cheryl had said when she called.

Not much.

I don't know why she even gives a shit.

Don't fish for compliments, I said, before reminding him that all this had resulted in my having to see him in the bathtub. You were married eight years. Of course she'd call.

Nine. Can you believe that?

No, I said, and must have laughed a little too authentically, because Barry made a big show of glaring at me.

Okay, tough guy, he said.

The phrase threw me back—any time Barry was challenged, it was *okay, tough guy*. We were 20 or 21; it was fall, he had just bought his first pumpkin truck, and I was working for him doing fall cleanups, as I did a few times. He was standing in the bed of the truck, walking on the leaves to pack them down, and I told him my old hockey coach could get me on the police if I could get through the academy. He stopped stomping, but for only a half step. Okay, tough guy, he'd said. Go fight crime in a town with zero crime.

And that's what I did. We settled into our identities in town from then on: landscaper and cop, worn jeans for him, pressed blues for me. That identity didn't seem to work out too well for him, but mine was fine, although police work had never been a calling. A few years slid past and I kept being a cop more than anything, even though whenever I put on the uniform I felt like I was watching my own hands dressing someone else.

Terri had seen a genuine light in my eyes when I talked about other dreams. I wanted my own business. I had little storms of excitement planning each one, sketching logos on cocktail napkins at our bar: maybe do some masonry, learn furniture making at that school in Boston, take out loans and flip houses.

And then the idea that lit up Terri's eyes as well: starting a small farm together. We'd get excited after a couple beers, ride the high and pocket the notes I'd scribbled of her narration. Then a couple more beers as we moved on to usual stuff: who was sleeping with who, who had moved into the city, Bruins in the winter, Sox in the summer. I'd find the note crumpled in my pocket the next day, a dream from myself to myself, and all I could ever think about in those sober moments were the risks.

5

Barry and I heard the crash outside. We looked out the window and there was Cheryl, getting out of her little green Honda, which she had plowed into the front left fender of Barry's truck.

Fuck me! Barry yelled and ran for the door. I ran out with him.

Outside, the former Mr. and Mrs. Barry Tuck slid into the old routine with remarkable skill and flair. They danced around each other, Barry hugging his truck and Cheryl kicking gravel on his feet like a manager arguing with an umpire. As Barry flailed and protested, it was clear there wasn't any anger behind it. He looked relieved. And he never took his eyes off Cheryl.

But when Cheryl started yelling where is it? Where is it?—and refused to acknowledge me when I asked what she was talking about—the charm of the scene wore off, and I stepped between them. I pinned Cheryl's arms to her sides. I told her to be quiet a moment, and then she could yell if she still wanted to.

She glared at me. Yes, officer, sir. Of course, Officer Mills.

Barry, I said, Are you going to hurt yourself?

For fuck's sake.

Answer the question, Barry. So Cheryl can hear. Are you?

No.

Cheryl, are you going to take care of the damage to Barry's truck?

No, the big dumb asshole can't pick up his goddamn phone. You pick up Liz Garkowski's calls?

At this I began to usher Cheryl to her car.

This again! Barry yelled. Mills, did Terri ever insist you did some shit you didn't do?

Irrelevant, Barry.

Mills didn't do shit, Cheryl said. Terri wanted Jeff Zoppo, you big ape.

Thank you, Cheryl, I said. Lovely. Keep it moving.

Cheryl had it half right. It wasn't Jeff Zoppo. But Terri had fallen away from me. I hadn't done anything. I just went grayer to her, and grayer.

They made out at the bar *once*, Barry said, and everyone blew it up into this big fucking thing. Zoppo's in Arizona, for Christ's sake.

I almost had Cheryl to the car when she stopped and pushed back hard against me.

You know what, Barry, forget Liz Garkowski. Look at this fucking place. Cheryl stepped back and made a big sweep of her arm that first drew our eyes to the oil puddles and the crumpled cars, then the caged shop windows and greasy vinyl siding, and finally to the small, closed window of Barry's kitchen, tucked in the eaves. Is this what you think of yourself?

Barry yelled that it was, and then turned away from us, his back hunched. He didn't need to consider the question.

Cheryl, watched him, sad and resigned, exhaustion in her eyes.

I can't take it anymore, Mills. Wake the fuck up, you know?

I know, Cheryl, I said. I know.

And I heard Terri saying, You have to take a *chance,* hon.

Barry had composed himself. Thanks for coming, Cheryl. I'm blown away by your concern.

Easy, Barry, I said.

Barry, you fat shit, go take a drive by Mills' house and see how a man lives who has some respect for himself.

At this, I stuffed Cheryl into her car as if she was going in the back of a cruiser. She let out a little grunt and looked up at me, surprised by the force.

She was about to ramp it up again but I cut her off.

Cheryl, shut up and go home. I slammed the door.

Barry came around me, jamming himself between me and Cheryl. He poked me in the chest.

Don't you dare talk to her like that.

6

Back upstairs, I set some water to boil—but Barry didn't have any coffee or tea, so I shut it off. I wanted to make sure he was calm.

Can you believe she actually called it in?

She was worried, I said. And I thought about Terri, how there was no way she would sob to the police about suicide if I didn't answer her calls. But Terri didn't call at all.

She thought I friggin *killed* myself, he said. Think about that. I'm behind on the oil bill, but Jesus, you know? What did she think, I was going to shoot myself?

I lied and said no. I didn't want to get into it. Then I remembered that Cheryl owned a gun. Barry had bought it for her protection after she kicked him out. I taught her to shoot it at the police range. Cheryl had been screaming: *where is it, where is it.*

I didn't want to stay, and it was getting dark outside. Barry was quiet, looking out the window, and then at his phone on the nightstand, then back out the window.

I said, Barry, you ok?

Yeah.

I looked at the breadbox on the table behind Barry. He'd stood in front of it the whole time I was there, and he was a guy that never stood when there was a seat available.

Alright, then I'm going. I moved toward him. I'm just going to grab a piece of bread, something. I haven't eaten.

There's none in there, he said, turning. I saw his hands grip the edge of the table, and there was a sort of defiant fear in his eyes.

I'm just going to check, I said, looking at him squarely, and he knew I knew.

After a moment he said fuck it, then pushed off the table and threw himself onto the bed. He flipped the TV on, loud canned laughter that he turned down.

I lifted the little garage door of the breadbox, pulled the plastic-bagged white bread out with a crinkle, and saw the leather-brown handle of Cheryl's gun. I slid it in my belt at my back. I undid the twisty around the neck of the bag and removed a piece of bread, put the piece in my mouth, then re-twisted the bag, replaced it in the breadbox, and lowered the door.

Barry had switched to a cooking show, the sizzle of onions or peppers hitting the pan.

You know, I always felt badly for you, he said. In that monkey suit, the dopey hat, busting minivans for running yellow lights, chasing stoned high school kids out of the woods.

And then Barry let loose, about me taking every odd job in town, fixing screen doors and putting in slop sinks. You know why guys pick up extra shifts? For the *money*, you dumb shit; but you're not paying tuition, you're not buying any rings, you don't even go on vacation. Why don't you go cut your lawn for the fifth time this week? You're the town handyman because you're a fucking joke.

And I let him go on, and I thought of the exhaustion on Cheryl's face. *Wake the fuck up, you know?* I think Barry knew that this time, this blowout—with the gun involved—was too much for Cheryl. He'd actually lost her. No more calls.

You think you're so fucking tidy in that little house of yours. Cutting stripes in your lawn, the cutesy brick walk, fresh coat of asphalt sealer on the driveway every spring. Nice and neat for you and nobody.

And you keep this place a dump for you and nobody.

I'd bit, and Barry started nodding. He scooted up in the bed. You know what makes us different, Millsy?

Shock me, Barry.

A fucking vacuum cleaner.

I wanted to toss the gun on the pillow next to him. We can rake our own leaves. But he was right. A clean house isn't self-respect. It's self-politeness. It's civility. The biggest risks were a crack in the asphalt or dust on the dresser.

I have to ask you again, are you going to hurt yourself?

Barry scooted back and turned his attention to the show. He said it quietly: The moment has passed.

I believed him. I had the gun. And even though I didn't know how serious the whole thing had been, I felt I'd been around death in some way, to some extent, and some dark vapor of it was still tucked away in between those boxes.

The worry lines on Barry's forehead seemed deeper, and his gray eyes darkened now as the outside light dimmed, getting low enough to justify switching on one of his three or four lamps, which I did. I closed the door on my way out.

7

Nothing happened the rest of the night, and I thought about these Friday and Saturday late shifts—I wasn't helping out the young cops with kids or the old cops who'd lost the legs for it. I'd partially admitted this to myself for a while now. Just like the worn windows I'd replaced, the crumbly chimneys I'd repointed, the rotted decks I'd ripped off and reframed. I was filling time.

I decided to take the cruiser home for the night, not wanting to go back to the station. I pulled in at about three in the morning and sat in the driveway and looked at my house, neat as a pin. No one could ever commit suicide in a house that neat.

I walked across the grass to the center of my front yard.

I could see the outline of the couch through the front window where Terri had sat me down and confessed that her eye had been wandering, and I was too good a man to cheat on. She apologized for kissing Jeff in the bar. She said she couldn't get past her belief that I would never give myself a real shot at achieving anything that meant something to me. Instead, I'd remain a cop, stay in a house I'd never liked, and, most relevant to her, turn any conversation about what was important to me into a petty fight about something else. I loved her more than ever in that moment for knowing me so well. I reached out for her arm, and she let me touch it before gently pulling it into her lap.

I asked her to stay the night and found myself choking on the words, knowing she wouldn't. I remembered thinking, *she doesn't want you anymore*, and I didn't want someone who didn't, but just barely.

I felt hollow and desperate now, and thought of how silent it was in my house, the bare workbench in the basement, the empty beer cans re-boxed and awaiting recycling, the bagged bowling ball stuffed in the hall closet, the hockey gear somewhere in the attic, and the enormous fucking bed, the sheets pulled tight as they would go.

I took the Tucks' gun from my waistband and looked at it in the moonlight. My gun had never felt real. I'd never considered reaching for it. But this gun had weight and menace. It looked hungry, alive in my palm. As if it really had killed Barry.

I wondered how close Barry had come. If the muzzle had touched his temple, or the whiskers of his throat. If he'd had it cocked. I wondered how he could have been listening to glam rock and scrubbing his armpits so energetically after. Maybe he'd just taken the gun to scare Cheryl, get her to call.

What is it that stops you from answering the phone and puts a gun in your hand? I wondered if I'd ever been close to being close, if it had ever been just beyond my periphery. Maybe that thing was waiting inside my house, hiding in vacuumed carpets, gripping the underside of scrubbed refrigerator shelves, lingering in the shadows of the few boxes of Terri's items she'd left in the basement, the cardboard gone soft from the cement floor.

I looked into the night. Maybe God really had called for Barry. Some darkness seemed to stand next to me then and I gave a half check over my shoulder. Nothing but perfectly manicured grass. Maybe He was calling me now.

I pictured that movie scene, a disgraced Army general dressing up in his blues, polishing his medals, leaving a tidy enveloped note on a dustless desk before removing a gun from the top drawer.

I thought of the Big Talk again, remembering more of what

Terri had said, about hunger and risk and hope. Challenges I hadn't wanted to hear, ideas that had felt irrelevant to her having fallen out of love with me.

I pictured Terri in the hardware store again. Comfortable smile and strong arms. She'd become fully herself, alive, the same brightness to her eyes and skin as those times we had planned the farm. The same brightness I had felt in my own eyes. The same life as when she jumped on my back and kissed my neck when I showed her the plot of land I'd found.

I pictured the farm stand she was building, imagined pulling my cruiser onto the grass across the street. Terri, giving change to a woman and her daughter, as a guy about my build bagged lettuce and carrots and an eggplant. The red farm stand doors, swung open, and a chalkboard hung on the inside, Terri's neat handwriting on it—prices for zucchini and tomatoes, corn and garlic. Above that was the farm's logo: planting lines converging at a horizon, *Sunrise Farm* arched across the sky, drawn in my hand.

In her chalk handwriting I read the last lines of the note I'd torn up and forgotten:

*Wake up tomorrow. Wake up.*
*Listen to You.*
*Don't leave it in your mind.*
*I love you,*
*Terri*

I was scared to bring the gun in the house with me. I walked around to the backyard and lay down in the grass, looking up. I placed Cheryl's gun at my side and drifted off, dreamt again of a farm, high in the clouds, this time harvesting pumpkins. Again, Terri was with me. I dreamt about the call I'd received that day—the boxes in Barry's apartment, Barry and Cheryl screaming at each other. And as I slept, that call came to me over the radio again and again, blipping with static before I heard any voices—and it became a different sort of call after all the repetition throughout the night. And when I woke the next day, the sunlight waking me early, only my thin police uniform separating my body from the soil, it had become a call I could begin to answer.

# *Saliva Terracade*

## *by Vi Khi Nao*

Your tongue is lightweight
Like ceramic tiles
While you lick
Your lover in order to
Build a saliva-based
Terracade
You may be Shane
Henrik, Australian,
Architect, building
Your cubistic blocks
But Picasso beats
You to it without
Resorting to enzyme
Lubrication, bacterial
Decay or mucosal
Refusal, and the
Submandibular Gland is
Simply a glance away

# *Going Back to Denmark: Landscape and Memory*

*by Cathy Schen*

*Vilhelm Hammershøi "Interior With A Reading Lady" (1900). Image from Wikiart.*

1.

Denmark has a sense of smallness, of boundedness. That was my initial impression as an American returning to a childhood home after forty years. The country consists of an archipelago of islands and a peninsula, Jutland, its largest land mass, that peaks above the continent like a hand with a delicate wrist connecting it to the body. Ocean borders the land at all sides; the only country accessible by land via this narrow isthmus is Germany. In addition to the delimitation by water, a border of darkness closes in around the country during the long winter season. From November until March, the sky is overcast and gray, a veil hiding the sun from view. This muted daylight yields to complete dark by early afternoon. The Danes have adapted to the darkness by creating light and warmth in their interior, domestic spaces. The Danish word hyggelig means cordial, heartfelt, hospitable, suggesting cozy evenings indoors with good company, sheltered from the damp cold.

The Danes also cope with the northern winter by making the most of spring and summer. In beach clubs along the coast, nude, segregated sunbathing decks exist for men and women, banks of bodies of all shapes and ages lying outside, taking in hours of sunshine with an occasional cooling swim in the interior ocean pool.

In the center of Copenhagen, a formal park called Kongens Have (King's Garden) attracts families, couples, and friends who emerge from their dwellings on foot or by bike, laden with baskets. They spread out their blankets on the grass to make outdoor living rooms. I watched two prepubescent girls, blonde and chubby, wriggle out of their undergarments into bikinis with only the smallest towels wrapped around their bodies for cover, while my husband and I camped for a nap, jet-lagged and waiting to check into our hotel.

Despite the natural boundaries of sea and dark, the level landscape and omnipresent ocean create a distant horizon that carries the eye out as far as it can see. One can easily imagine this vista enticing the Danes out on their Viking voyages a thousand years ago, driven by ambition and the scarcity of farmland for its population. For a person returning to a childhood home, this vista draws out the soul and beseeches it to search out that other faraway place, of lost homes, of past memories.

2.

Denmark was the home of my mother's ancestors. My mother's maiden name was Hansen, a common Danish name. Yet, for me, Denmark represents my father, and holds memories of him and me when I was nine and ten years old. Those were years I identified with him, wore a cowgirl outfit with a cap pistol at each hip, and was, to my recollection, like those well-fed Danish girls, relatively free and unselfconscious.

Esso Chemical transferred my father to Denmark. It was the start of his international career, his first overseas job as project manager in charge of constructing a plastics factory in Roskilde. We moved to an unfinished house at the end of a street that began in town and ended in a country field. A half-hour commute from Copenhagen, Roskilde, the former capital of Denmark a thousand years ago, was reawakening as one of Denmark's industrial centers. As I write this, I look up at a photograph I have pinned above my desk from those years. It is a 3 x 2-inch rectangle that shows my father and myself sitting on a banquette side by side in a restaurant. I am holding a chicken drumstick in my hand, smiling at the person across the table, my face turned slightly toward my father but not looking directly at him. My inner elbow touches his; his face is turned toward mine. My father's outside hand softly cups his left cheek. The sun streams through the stained glass window behind us and casts its light on my father, who is smiling at me as I, unaware, bask in his gaze.

*Vilhelm Hammershøi "The Tall Windows" (1913).*

This photograph depicts something about my years in Denmark. It captures one of those moments invisible to us when we were experiencing them, both because they were not in our literal view, as in this photograph, and because we were too young to grasp their significance. It proves that we can profit from experiences that are outside our awareness. It also signifies that my return to this country had something to do with reclaiming those years and the relationship with my father—that I needed to return to bring it all into focus, apart from all that came later.

3.

Roskilde seemed to suit my father perfectly, with his penchant for water and his inner dualism of rural life and industrial ambition. This was not so for my mother. Roskilde was still a provincial town in the 1960s, with very few English-speaking people. My mother, unable to speak Danish, must have been lonely there with no one to talk to but her young children. After a year in Roskilde, she asked my father to move closer to Copenhagen, so that she could be part of the expatriate community there. Charlottenlund, an affluent suburb of Copenhagen, became our next home.

4.

The day after my husband and I arrived in Denmark, we made our first trip to Charlottenlund. We mounted our black rental bicycles and pulled out into the stream of fast-paced commuters biking into the center city. Women sat tall and upright on their bikes, wearing skirts and high heels, and pedaling so briskly that I found myself passed until I relaxed and picked up the pace. Men whisked by dressed in business suits, briefcases strapped across their chests or clipped onto the rear bike rack. We turned left off the bicycle highway to pass along Copenhagen's large lakes, the Sankt Jorgens So, Peblinge So, and Sortedams So. A few joggers went by, and people walking their dogs. We travelled the breadth of the city, starting from the east, and reached the western district of

Osterport (West City). There, we turned onto a bustling commercial boulevard that headed north to the coastal suburbs. We cycled past the giant green beer bottle that marked the entrance to the Tuborg beer factory.

The Milanese man from whom we'd rented our bicycles had scoffed when we told him we were going to Charlottenlund. "There's nothing there," he said. "That's where the fancy-pants live."

"I used to live in Charlottenlund," I explained, "and so we're going to see the house where I grew up." It hadn't seemed fancy to me back then.

My mother had given me the name of the street where we'd lived: Prince Elvinsvej. We located the street on my husband's iPad. Its pulsing green dot indicated that we were approaching our destination. The day was hot. The sky was blue and cloudless, and on our right, the ocean glinted between the apartment buildings. I watched the street signs tick by on our left. When I saw the street sign Maglemosevej, I called out to my husband. This was not the street my mother had identified, but it flashed as familiar.

"That's it! I remember now! Maglemosevej! We have to turn around!" I stopped and swung my bike around, not waiting for my husband.

"Are you sure?" my husband called, still pedaling ahead, reluctant to backtrack, not trusting the reliability of childhood memory.

"Yes, yes, I'm sure." I dismounted and pulled my bicycle to the crosswalk and pressed the signal button to cross the street. And I *was* sure. The street's name had risen up out of my forgotten memory, its sound rolling easily on my tongue. I remembered the black walnut tree in the backyard then, and the plum tree that dropped its dark purple fruit on the grass.

*Vilhelm Hammershøi "The Sunny Parlor" (1901).*

5.

Marion Milner, in her book *On Not Being Able to Paint*, ponders the claim that painting is concerned with feelings about space. Space is emotionally laden, Milner says, when we consider it from the perspective of the young child who must reach for a mother's arms. Space holds the feelings of being apart or united, of being hungry or replete. As much as painters grapple with color and line and form, distance and perspective, they are also capturing in paint early feelings of separation and togetherness.

I live in a watery enclave west of Boston, part of the Sudbury River watershed. What I'd never noticed until I returned from Denmark was how closely I had replicated the flat, open, water-soaked environment of that country in my adult surroundings. I had chosen a place that, without my realizing it, was physically similar to where I had grown up.

6.

When my husband and I cycled down Maglemosevej, I spotted the house easily. Its red walls and black timbered framing were distinct and recognizable to me. Since no one was home, I peeked in the windows. I opened the side gate and took a quick stroll in the backyard. I walked around to the far side and looked up for my bedroom window. For the first time, I realized the house resided in a well-to-do neighborhood.

Peering in the kitchen window, I remembered the smell of my mother cooking dog food for our new puppy. I saw in my mind's eye the round table in the basement set for a tea party for all my stuffed animals. This was the year I jealously and repeatedly hid my younger sister's blankie. I attended a French Catholic school, where I wore a stiff and scratchy uniform—a woolen pleated skirt that pinched my middle and a thick linen sailor blouse covered by a navy blue polyester pinafore. I pushed a boy out of a tree and he broke his arm. I snacked on Bugles while reading and got a little chubby. I was in fourth grade.

These less pleasant memories, not difficult to recover, were not, I felt, what had motivated my return to Denmark. I had not come to unearth unhappiness, but to find something else, something I had loved and lost. Another memory arose. I remembered gathering a huge basket of yellow-green cherries from the scrubby forests of Roskilde. I brought them home for my mother, who mistook the cherries as raw or poisonous and threw them away. I had always felt aggrieved that I never got to taste them. Did they symbolize what I was trying to find?

And so, on our next day in Denmark, my husband and I boarded the commuter train at Central Station in Copenhagen, bikes in tow. We arrived in Roskilde and headed off to the outskirts, where our map indicated we'd find Pristemarkevej, the other street where I'd once lived. We biked along a commercial strip lined with gas stations and small businesses. We found Pristemarkevej and turned left onto the street. Right away, at the second house, I told my husband to stop. "I *think* this is it," I said, but without the conviction of the day before.

The house was red brick, modest, with a picture window at the front and the main door along the side. We took pictures, and then rode further up the street, passing identical brick homes along the way. I spotted a thatched roof farmhouse surrounded by a high stucco wall. Another brick home stood across from it, somewhat larger than the others, but still unpretentious. "This *must* be it," I said, and took more pictures. The house was unoccupied, but turning to look at the farmhouse, I caught a glimpse of a boy at the window upstairs, watching us. He pulled away when I looked up. I stood by the gate and called out. The boy came down, and gestured that no one was home. I smiled, and explained my situation in English—"I used to live here!"

The boy shook his head, not understanding.

I waved goodbye, a gesture that belonged to my fondness for my old neighbors back then. We got on our bikes and rode to the end of the street, past open fields. We headed on toward the fjord and stopped for a swim. Afterward, we biked back toward town, taking a narrow, sandy trail along the shoreline that wove in and out of the small dunes and then cut back into agricultural fields. As we bumped along on our bikes, we passed a small grove of trees. There, hanging in clusters, were the yellow cherries of my memory. I called out to my husband, "Stop! I found something!" I propped my bike against the tree trunk, plucked the cherries and ate them confidently. "Delicious!" I pronounced.

My husband followed suit, and the two of us chewed and spit out pits, laughing as juice dripped down our chins. Eating those cherries felt like I was being given back something I had loved, larger than the cherries, embracing a whole landscape. Now the physical and sensual enjoyment of finding, gathering, and eating them was tremendously enlivening. I thought to myself, *See? I was right, they* are *good.*

As she draws, Marion Milner asks herself if her refusal to follow the rules of a single observing eye and formal principles of perspective is a denial of her separateness in the world. She decides that no, it is not a retreat from this fact of existence. Rather, she finds that painting, when it is alive, creates a relation with objects that is based on other senses besides the sense of seeing, and allows that we are more mixed up with the external world than common sense or visual perspective allows. Milner concludes that painting "felt more like a search, a going backwards perhaps, but a going back to look for something, something that could have real value for adult life if only it could be recovered."

7.

The day I wrote about these cherries, I was talking to my college age son on the phone. "Mom, remember that time you didn't want me to make homemade tortillas?"

"No, I don't remember that," I replied. "Did I?"

"Yeah, you did," my son insisted. "I think it was because we were having guests for dinner or something. Anyway, I went over to a friend's house yesterday and we made them from scratch. They were easy and really good!"

He too had gone back to recover something that had been lost, something he could use going forward in his adult life.

8.

On our last day in Denmark, my husband and I decided to visit my Charlottenlund home again and afterward go to a museum nearby. We paused at the house briefly. It had a neglected and empty feeling. We rode on.

The Ordrupgaard Museum was on a quiet residential street. The gravel crunched beneath our bikes as my husband and I rode up the drive. A gracious country estate stood before us, the former home of Wilhelm and Henny Hansen, avid art collectors at the turn of the twentieth century. Since the museum wasn't open yet, we parked and locked our bikes and followed a path around the side of the house to a formal garden. An enormous oak tree shaded the garden's south side. Clipped hedges bordered the pea stone walks and rose gardens. My husband wandered off to sketch, and I lay down under the tree and closed my eyes. The breeze lifted the leaves and they rustled softly, a summer sound, a childhood enchantment.

9.

In paintings that depict domestic interiors—that are spare, architectural, monochrome, that draw the eye to lines suggestive of eternity, of wall and ceiling, of open doorways, that are barren of any evidence of nature—the Danish painter Vilhelm Hammershøi (1864-1916) creates an atmosphere of intimacy and contemplative expansiveness. It's like when one hikes up a mountain and, with a sharp in-breath, takes in the silence and wilderness at the summit. A cupboard, a blue and white porcelain bowl feel evocative, like portraits of significance.

I came upon these paintings as a personal, shocking, exhilarating discovery. When my husband and I left to go back to the United States, I took home with me a new love—a painter and his paintings.

*Vilhelm Hammershøi "Portrait of Ida Ilsted, Later the Artist's Wife" (1890). Image from Statens Museum for Kunst, smk.dk.*

10.

Rainer Maria Rilke was twenty-nine when he discovered Hammershøi's paintings. Rilke was on his way to Sweden and stopped in Dusseldorf, Germany, for the International Art Exhibition. There he saw Hammershøi's portrait of Ida, Hammershøi's wife. It is one of Hammershøi's few full-face portraits. In it, Ida wears a plain black dress and loose brown jacket. Apart from a gold wedding band, a gray feather in her hat is Ida's only adornment. Her face glows, wistful and tender. Her eyes are pensive, turned inward. The light emanating from her face contrasts with the dark expanse of dress that forms a heavy triangle below. In her lap rest her two unclasped hands, their fingers furled, or maybe slightly clenched, ambiguous as to whether she has just let something go or is refusing to grasp on. The two empty hands and their separateness are suggestive. Our eye is drawn back to the painting's brightest focus, her face. There we find the painting's only vibrant color—a touch of rose on Ida's lips and cheeks.

11.

When Rilke arrived in Sweden, he made several trips to Copenhagen in order to see more of Hammershøi's work. Skåne, or southern Sweden, is visible from Copenhagen across the Øresund strait. For Rilke, it would have been a short ferry voyage. Nowadays, one can drive across by taking a bridge and tunnel thoroughfare that connects Copenhagen to Malmö, Sweden. From a distance, cars can be seen leaving Denmark and traveling along a bridge that goes right into the ocean. The bridge ends abruptly and the cars seem to vanish in a haze of reflecting light. Flying into Copenhagen, my husband and I observed this mystery during our descent.

Later, we learned that this was the famous Øresundsbroen that links the two countries. Danes consider southern Sweden an easy weekend excursion; for us, it had seemed a glistening path to the unknown.

12.

Rilke never wrote the essay on Hammershøi as he'd intended. Instead, Rilke travelled on to Paris, where he studied Cezanne's paintings and named this latter painter, in 1906, as a formative influence on his poetry. In a letter of apology to Alfred Bramsen, the Danish host who had opened his private collection for Rilke's viewing, Rilke wrote:

> *"There is no hurry, it seems to me. Hammershøi is not one of those artists that one needs to talk about* quickly. *His work is long and slow and at whatever moment one comes to grips with it, one will have ample occasion to speak of what is significant and essential in art."*

13.

When I returned from Denmark, I went to the Fine Arts Library at Harvard University and took out art books on Hammershøi. I lugged the heavy books back and forth to my office and the Concord library, places where I like to write. I took them to bed with me and propped them up on pillows. I turned the pages and gazed at these paintings with satisfaction. It was as if Hammershøi's paintings served as a bridge to my new self that came home from Denmark. I felt as though I was gathering pieces of my lost Danish childhood.

Anne-Birgitte Fonsmark, the director of Ordrupgaard, says that Hammershøi's paintings can be regarded as a series of existential statements. Hammershøi was interested in empty interior spaces and distilling the essence from a room or object, in a manner one would call poetic. The phenomenologist Gaston Bachelard, in his book *The Poetics of Space*, writes about the intimacy of roundness, the mystery of cupboards, the soul of the domestic interior.

14.

Anna Freud, in a 1947 letter to her friend and colleague August Aichhorn, mourned not being able to return to Vienna, her childhood home. Her refusal to go back was mixed with grief and protest. Her father, Sigmund Freud, had died on September 23, 1939, and all four of her elderly aunts had died in concentration camps. She wrote:

*"I would like so much for one to tell you of my father's last weeks and days, and what it means for me to live without him. I would also like to tell you what leaving Vienna has meant to me and how strange it is to carry a past within oneself which can no longer be built upon."*

I was touched by how Anna Freud joined the loss of her father with that of her childhood home. I felt her pain of being unable to make the journey back, felt how a landscape and a home can be connected with one's father. Even though my father died long after we left Denmark, looking back at those years now, I realize how much I felt myself as my father's little girl back then, happy in his company.

Later, when we moved from Denmark to Holland, I left childhood for the teenage years. My parents started to fight and my father began to drink excessively. The girls, including me, shifted over to my mother's side. My father became less known and more distant.

15.

Can a painting capture these feelings? Hammershøi was a reserved man. He and his wife never had children. They lived a quiet life with the artist's mother. In all my reading, there is very little mention of Hammershøi's father.

16.

It is strange how the unconscious works. When I first described

Denmark's landscape as looking like a hand, I thought that I was seeing something quite literal, an actual resemblance to a physical hand. Now, having come to this place in my writing, I realize that I've been contemplating hands and noting their appearance for some time. This preoccupation of mine is all about separation and togetherness. Holding hands is part of the story. Like the feelings of space in painting, hands—whether painted images, literary descriptions, or the flesh-and-blood real ones—embody primal feelings about being held and being apart.

17.

When my father was dying, I was left alone with him while my sisters and stepmother went out to get lunch. My father had been sleeping, half in and half out of consciousness all day. In the silence of the room, he awoke. He asked me to prop him up against the pillow. I leaned over and slipped my arms around his chest and under his armpits so that we were chest to chest, and then I heaved him up against the headboard. I sat back down, closer to him this time, right alongside him. He reached out for my hand and I grasped his in mine. His hand was warm and large and could still enfold mine in his.

He became surprisingly alert and lucid then, and started speaking as if the course of his life was passing through him. He spoke of his work, his love for his current wife and for his three daughters. He told me how he knew our mother loved all three of us, too. I heard him, but with only half an ear, because I was swept by a tremendous surge of feeling. It felt as if we were, as Milner might say, very mixed up with each other at that moment. We were pausing together at the threshold between my father's life and his death. I felt as if he was giving me his love, and I was giving him mine, so that I could endure his death and so he could have me with him on his next passage. His hand holding mine was the conduit.

18.

Almost a year has passed. It was August when my husband and I traveled to Denmark and spent a week there. Now, it is May, and summer is approaching. Spring has been distinctly Scandinavian with overcast, raw, rainy days. Sunlight appears briefly, luxuriously, then is stolen away. I long for heat. I realize I've spent a year relinquishing my past afresh.

My younger son heard that I was writing about my childhood in Denmark and asked me to send him what I'd written. I did so with trepidation. I didn't know if it would feel weird for him to read about his mom's personal life. He called me up a few days after I emailed him my work in progress. I could hear a kind of crunch, crunch in the background. Probably, I thought, he was walking to dinner, one of his favorite times to call.

"I never knew this about you, Mom," he said. "It made me realize how *much* I don't know about your childhood. I like how you portrayed your character in the story. And I really like how you portrayed Dad. Your tag-along."

My son helped me understand how important the character of my husband, the tag-along, was to my journey searching for my lost childhood home. In fairy tales, the seeker sets out alone, but companions join along the way. Without these companions, the quest would not succeed. These new relationships are in themselves part of achieving the goal. The seeker shares her dream with others. In my case, one such companion was my husband. Others were my sons, who now knew a little more about their mother. And, finally, Hammershøi. With his paintings, I didn't return empty handed.

19.

Since the only Hammershøi painting in public view in the United States was at the Museum of Fine Arts in Boston, I went there. I inquired at the visitor information center and was directed to Gallery 252 on the second floor. Coming up the wide marble staircase, I felt a sudden sadness come over me, as if I was about to say goodbye to a long lost love. Entering the gallery room, I glanced left. Tucked in a corner, in the shadow of a mahogany cabinet, hung Hammershøi's *Woman in an Interior, 1909*. Just under two feet by two feet, the painting seemed small, dark, and a little forlorn. The green of the central paned window held the only color amongst somber browns and beiges of the interior. The painting was barren of material possessions. I felt a little disappointed.

Leaving the room, I moved next door. In this gallery, two of Cezanne's paintings hung side by side. I was stunned by the thick vibrant dabs of paint. I felt a sudden visceral joy.

*Vilhelm Hammershøi "Woman in an Interior" (1909). Image from www.mfa.org.*

*Unless noted otherwise, images are from Wikimedia Commons*

# *Nil Nisi of the Dead*

## *by Len Krisak*

*—variously attributed to Diogenes and Chilon*

1.
*Nothing but good*: that's what I've always read.
They never met *her.* All the papers said
How loving, loved, admired, and esteemed
She was. A paragon—or so it seemed.
But they weren't there the day I heard her say
How pushy was that Jew to get his way.
Of course she said it underneath her breath.
Now everyone can celebrate her death.

2.
So feisty, yet so loveable and warm:
A mensch who stood for every good reform
(Left undefined). That's how the papers saw
Him—gruff but kind. He'd rarely rub you raw,
Unless to get his way. *Then* he would let it out—
No trace of modest calm or grace or doubt—
And twist his visage in a bully's rage
They missed on the obituary page.

# *Speak Up, I'm Eavesdropping*

## *by Barbara Rogan*

I put it off as long as I could. Covered up, as people do; I smiled and nodded. Finally, I gave in and went to an audiologist.

She sat me in a booth and covered my head with large earphones. I could see her through the window, taking notes. If there was a period of silence, I watched her face for clues. It was a test, after all; I wanted to do well.

Afterward, we went over the results. "Mild hearing loss," she said cheerfully. "Comes with age. You probably don't even notice it except when you're trying to have a conversation somewhere noisy."

I didn't mind so much about conversations. One can always shout. But noisy public places are prime eavesdropping territory, and for a writer that matters terribly.

Writers are nosy. I say this without apology, as nosiness is a requirement of the trade. For writers, as for actors, observation fuels invention. Our natural state is that of a fly on the wall, our patron saint Harriet the Spy.

As both human nature and language are the proper study of

writers, eavesdropping is not a trivial pursuit. It's a means of staying in touch with the ever-evolving vernacular and transcending our narrow personal circles. Hearing in general is so vital to writers that deaf writers are as rare on the ground as deaf musicians; yet some degree of hearing loss is almost inevitable with age. The first time I heard about Sheryl Sandberg's *Lean In*, I thought someone had finally come up with a practical solution, cheaper than hearing aids, though limited in efficacy; there's only so much you can lean in without landing in someone's soup.

Eavesdropping has always been a rich and essential resource for me. I once spent 36 hours in a Brooklyn ER with my younger son waiting for a bed to open up. Despite my anxiety, I spent that time doing what writers do: observing and listening. And even before my son was released, I knew that I'd found the perfect setting for a book I'd long wanted to write.

It's not just me. There's a reason, apart from coffee, why so many writers work in cafés: they're great places to eavesdrop. Buses, trains, waiting rooms , and bleachers are all excellent resources, but my personal favorite was always the diner. The booths provide enough illusory privacy to encourage revealing conversation, enough real privacy to allow me to take notes. I've overheard break-ups and make-ups, quarrels and seductions, women dissecting men, men puzzling over women, doctors dishing about patients, cult recruiters exchanging tips. My favorite bit of found art was a conversation between a father and his young son.

"You know, Dad," the child said thoughtfully, "some of the best things in life are things you can't buy with money."

"Yes, my son?"

"Like friends," the boy said. "And a family that loves you. And picking your nose."

So I didn't take the audiologist's diagnosis well. Any degree of hearing loss threatened me where I lived; think of a painter with cataracts. Everything else aside, hearing loss is associated with encroaching old age, which has its own particular terrors for writers.

It's not discussed in polite circles, age being the last remaining closet. But the truth is that there are commercial penalties for WWO—Writing While Old. One is no longer in the running for "hot new writer." There is, sadly but inevitably, a tipping point at which the books become sexier than the author. Older writers in search of a new agent or publishing house are at a disadvantage compared to young writers with decades of work ahead of them.

Nor is hearing the only sense affected by age. Others may decline as well; yet fiction is grounded in sensory detail. A permanent dimming of sensation can force the older writer to resort to life's pale cousin, memory.

Physically, writing a novel is far more labor-intensive than most people think. To produce a manuscript of 100,000 words, the writer might easily type five times that many in drafts. Travel, too, becomes more onerous as writers age and commercial planes devolve into sardine cans—yet nothing is more nourishing for writers than travel.

For some aging writers, there is also anxiety. Writing doesn't come with a pension. This startling realization dawns on most writers around the time their non-writer friends begin retiring with comfortable nest eggs. No doubt it should have occurred to them sooner, but they were too busy reveling in the perks of their profession: setting their own hours, working at home, and making a living doing what they loved.

Fortunately, these drawbacks are offset by advantages that allow writers, unlike dancers or athletes, to continue playing at a high level even in old age. Experience is a great asset. One doesn't need 20/20 vision to see into the human heart, the wellspring of all fiction. Older writers have lived, learned, read, suffered, and survived more. "The afternoon knows what the morning never suspected," said Robert Frost, who kept writing well into his 80s.

Older writers have skills, because the good ones never stop growing. They tend to value simplicity and clarity over ostentation. They put the story first. They've found their voice.

The extreme turbulence of youth is behind them. When productivity is the goal, it's better to have suffered the slings and arrows of outrageous fortune than to be currently under fire.

Technology gives us tools as well. Google Earth is no substitute for travel, but it sure is a great backup. And writers afflicted with arthritis can now resort to first-rate dictation software.

Bottom line, it's not as if we have a choice. Writers write, whatever the circumstances. As for me, I'm making my adjustments. I thought of handing out cards—"Speak up, I'm eavesdropping"—but decided that might have an inhibiting effect. Instead, I practice leaning in, though I find it's not much needed. Recently in an airport departure lounge, I heard a young woman on a cell phone describe in excruciating detail the party she'd gone to the night before. She'd gotten wasted, she said, passed out, and woke the next morning in bed with a stranger. As the young woman strolled off, still spewing into her phone, a flash symposium broke out among the dozen or so stunned passengers within earshot.

I hate it that I don't hear as well as I used to. These days, though, people talk more loudly and openly than ever before. It's wonderful how things work out.

# Contributors

**Lesley Bannatyne** is an author who writes on Halloween. This essay comes from research she conducted on her most recent book, Halloween Nation. Behind the Scenes of America's Fright Night, which was a Bram Stoker Award finalist. Read more of her work at iskullhalloween.com

**Jessica Bozek** is the author of *The Tales* (Les Figues, 2013) and *The Bodyfeel Lexicon* (Switchback, 2009), as well as several chapbooks. She runs the Small Animal Project Reading Series, teaches writing at Boston University, and lives with her family in Cambridge.

**Lauren Camp** is the author of three collections, most recently *One Hundred Hungers* (Tupelo Press, 2016), which won the Dorset Prize. Her poems appear in *Muzzle, Linebreak, The Seattle Review, Beloit Poetry Journal* and elsewhere, and her work has been translated into Turkish, Mandarin and Spanish. Lauren is a Black Earth Institute Fellow and the producer/host of Santa Fe Public Radio's "Audio Saucepan," which melds global music with contemporary poetry. www.laurencamp.com.

**Scott Challener** is a doctoral candidate in English at Rutgers University. He is the recipient of a 2016 Massachusetts Cultural Council Individual Artist Fellowship. His work has appeared in *Lana Turner Journal, Gulf Coast, The Rumpus, Mississippi Review,* and elsewhere.

**Martin Chan** is currently working on his first poetry collection.

**Dana Crum** is author of the chapbook *Good Friday 2000* (Q Ave Press, 2014) and is a Callaloo Fellow. He won the Eva Jane Romaine Coombe Writer's Residency at The Seven Hills School, had residencies at the Vermont Studio Center and VCCA and received a fellowship from Virginia Commonwealth University. The *Paris Review Daily* profiled him in 2013. His poetry, fiction and nonfiction have appeared, or are forthcoming, in *Blackbird, American Short Fiction, African Voices, Carve Magazine, The Source, The Innisfree Poetry Journal, Killens Review of Arts & Letters* and other publications. NPR affiliate WBEZ 91.5 FM Chicago broadcast a dramatic reading of his short story "My Heavenly Father" as part of its *Stories on Stage* program.

**Rosalie Davis** teaches writing and literature to adults in Cambridge and Brookline, and recently completed a Master of Liberal Arts in Humanities English) at Harvard Extension. Her first short story, "When the Pears Are Ripe," placed 2nd in UNH's 2010 short fiction contest. A longtime Boston freelancer and former editor of Horticulture Magazine, she has ontributed to many other house and home publications.

**Shane Delaney** holds an MFA in creative writing from Lesley University n Boston and a BA in English from Bates College. He lives in Charlestown, Massachusetts.

**Carol Dine** Poet, memoirist and essayist, her books include *Orange Night* 2014), poems inspired and accompanied by the images of Holocaust urvivor Samuel Bak, *Van Gogh in Poems,* and a memoir, *Places in the Bone.* Her work has appeared in *Boulevard, Bitter Oleander, Lilith,* and *Salamander,* mong other journals. Carol has been a poet-in-resident at the MacDowell Colony, Yaddo, Ragdale, and the Virginia Center for the Arts. She teaches nemoir at Massachusetts College of Art & Design, Boston.

**Mitchell Krockmalnik Grabois** has had over thirteen-hundred of his poems and fictions appear in literary magazines in the U.S. and abroad. He has been nominated for numerous prizes, and was awarded the 2017 Cooranga Writers Centre Prize (Australia) for Fiction. His novel, *Two-Headed Dog,* based on his work as a clinical psychologist in a state hospital, s available for Kindle and Nook, or as a print edition. To see more of his vork, google Mitchell Krockmalnik Grabois. He lives in Denver.

**riya Gupta** is a family physician from Montreal. She feels fortunate to ave grown up in two cultures — Canadian and Indian. She is also grateful hat, when taking a policy writing class last year, her prof didn't force her o write about policy. She likes having opinions and making people laugh, ometimes simultaneously.

**Dina Hardy**—recipient of an MFA from the Iowa Writers' Workshop, a Stegner Fellowship from Stanford University, residencies in Spain and Wales, and a Pushcart Prize nomination—is the author of the chapbook elections from The World Book (Convulsive Editions). Her work has ppeared or is forthcoming in numerous journals, such as *Gulf Coast, ecomP magazinE, Typo, Transom, Prelude, H_NGM_N,* and *Ink Brick*. "She ves in Madrid, Spain. To learn more about Dina and her work, check out er website www.dinahardy.com

**Janice N. Harrington** is the author of three books of poetry: *Even the Hollow My Body Made Is Gone, The Hands of Strangers,* and the newly released *Primitive: The Art and Life of Horace H. Pippin.* She curates "A Space for Image," a blog on poetic imagery, and teaches creative writing at the University of Illinois.

**Margaret Kahn** is the author of *Children of the Jinn, In Search of the Kurds and Their Country* and the entry on Kurds in The Harvard Encyclopedia of American Ethnic Groups. Her short fiction has appeared in *Ararat, Iowa Woman, Kalliope, Crab Orchard Review,* and the Sunday magazine section of the *San Jose Mercury News*. She lives in northern California where she is working on a novel about American expatriates living in Egypt in the 1970's.

**Len Krisak's** most recent books are Rilke's *New Poems* (a complete translation) and *Afterimage* (original poems). With work in the *Hudson, Sewanee, PN, Antioch,* and *Southwest Reviews,* he is the recipient of the Robert Penn Warren, Richard Wilbur, and Robert Frost Prizes, and a four time champion on *Jeopardy!*

**Jim Krosschell** divides his life into three parts: growing up for 2[illegible] years, working in science publishing for 29 years, and now writing in Massachusetts and Maine. His essays are widely published; a collection of those Maine-themed was published in *One Man's Maine* (May 2017) by Green Writers Press. His book *Owls Head Revisited* was published in 201[illegible] by North Country Press.

**Marco Maisto** is a Pushcart nominee who studied at the Iowa Writers' Workshop. Now or soon, you can find poetry/comix/art/reviews in *Drunken Boat, The Colorado Review, The Offing, Electric Lit/Okey-Panky, TYPO, Timber, Fjords, Spry, Heavy Feather Review, small po[r]tions,* and other journals. He lives in NYC.

**Michelle McGurk** is is a former reporter, currently working in public policy. She is a graduate of Lesley University's low-residency MFA program in Creative Writing. She has been a semi-finalist for the James Jones First Novel Fellowship, a finalist for the Writing by Writers Tomales Bay fellowship, and long-listed for the DISQUIET Literary Prize in fiction. Her fiction has previously appeared in *The Journal* and *Cherry Tree.*

**Vi Khi Nao** holds an MFA in fiction from Brown University. Her poetry collection, *The Old Philosopher,* was the winner of 2014 Nightboat Poetry Prize. Her manuscript, *A Brief Alphabet of Torture,* won the 2016 Ronald Sukenick Innovative Fiction Contest. In Fall 2016, Coffee House Press will publish her novel *Fish in Exile.*

**Josh Neufeld** is a Brooklyn-based cartoonist known for his nonfiction narratives of political and social upheaval, told through the voices of witnesses. Neufeld has been a Knight-Wallace Fellow in journalism, an Atlantic Center for the Arts Master Artist, and a Xeric Award winner. His works include *A.D: New Orleans After the Deluge,* about Hurricane Katrina, and *The Influencing Machine: Brooke Gladstone on the Medi*a. www.JoshComix.com

**Barbara Rogan** is the author of eight novels and coauthor of several nonfiction books. Her latest novel, *A Dangerous Fiction,* is a mystery set in the publishing world, published by Viking Books/Penguin. She teaches fiction writing workshops online at www.nextlevelworkshop.com.

**Cathy Schen** is a Boston area psychiatrist and assistant professor-part-time at Harvard Medical School where she teaches psychiatry residents. She has written and published on topics ranging from mothers who leave their children behind, the ethics of writing about patients, the restorative aspects of farming, and Willa Cather's search for belonging.

**Mimi Schwartz** is the author of *When History is Personal,* forthcoming Spring 2018 from University of Nebraska Press, from which this essay is excerpted. She won the *Foreword Magazine* Award for Memoir in 2008 for *Good Neighbors, Bad Times — Echoes of My Father's German Village*. Other books include *Thoughts from a Queen-Sized Bed* and *Writing True, the Art and Craft of Creative Nonfiction* (co-editor Sondra Perl). Mimi's essays have appeared in *The Missouri Review, Agni, Creative Nonfiction, Fourth Genre, Calyx, Tikkun, Florida Review, Brevity, The Writer's Chronicle,* among others, and seven essays have been Notables in *Best American Essays*. She is Professor Emerita at Richard Stockton College of New Jersey and lives in Princeton, New Jersey.

**Jared Stanley** is a poet, writer and interdisciplinary artist living in Reno, Nevada. *Ears,* his third collection of poetry, is forthcoming in 2017. Recent writing has appeared in *The Offing, Literary Hub,* and *Triple Canopy.*

**Nadia Viswanath** is a Master in Public Administration student at the Harvard Kennedy School and a Master in Business Administration student at MIT Sloan School of Management. Previously, Nadia worked in agricultural development in Ethiopia and as a management consultant at McKinsey & Company.

**Jonathan Weinert** is the author of *In the Mode of Disappearance,* winner of the Nightboat Poetry Prize, *and Thirteen Small Apostrophes,* a chapbook. With Kevin Prufer, he is the editor of *Until Everything Is Continuous Again: American Poets on the Recent Work of W.S. Merwin.*

**Maisie Wiltshire-Gordon** is fascinated by how language works and the ways we put it to use. She is looking for answers through storytelling, philosophy, and everyday conversation. She is currently a graduate student in philosophy at Brandeis University and lives in Cambridge, MA.

## ABOUT PANGYRUS

*Pangyrus* is a Boston-based group of writers, editors, and artists with a new vision for how high-quality creative work can prosper online and in print. We aim to foster a community of individuals and organizations dedicated to art, ideas, and making culture thrive.

Combining Pangaea and gyrus, the terms for the world continent and whorls of the cerebral cortex crucial to verbal association, Pangyrus is about connection.

## INDEX by AUTHOR and GENRE

CPSIA information can be obtained
at www.ICGtesting.com
Printed in the USA
FFOW04n2131280218
45324203-45991FF

9 780997 91642